BAILING WATER

BAILING WATER

John Dempsey

Iriswhite Publishing
New York

Bailing Water

Iriswhite Publishing
New York

For information, visit
www.iriswhite.com

ISBN: 0-9711072-3-8
Library of Congress Control Number: 2003104267
FIRST EDITION

Printed in the United States of America

For Lisa, the only one that matters . . .

TABLE OF CONTENTS

– Table of Contents –

– Table of Contents –

BAILING WATER

ⅭᏒ IT'S LIKE THIS

it's like this:

the bookstore won't stock the Greek magazine
that printed me,

they also feel that the title
'drive past the sun' (to blow off the stock life)
is
pointlessly
abstract -

told me:
'bic pen gambling is a real shitty piece - full of egotism and
pretension (it's true) - hey
asshole,
you should change your outlook.'

said:
'we're just not interested in this kind of work - get the point?
stop submitting.'
(4 poems a week)

replied to my emails:
'this is not poetry.
this is barely English.
read
our featured authors and get an idea of what
REAL poetry
is all about.'

(excuse me,
sir -

by some chance -

is it unicorns and mountain landscape and Hollywood happy,
hand holding endings with rainbows and rhyming dictionary
story lines?

is it
Shakespeare type

knockoff?

hmm?)

but then again:
Vincent
was considered a madman
and

Nabakov
a pedophile . . .

politicians are the new genius
along with
leaders of military
and financial analysts - and I
want
no part
of that group . . .

it's like this Baby,
I think the small time
is about all the time
I
need.

❧ WOKE UP THIS MORNING

woke up this morning

and realized -

that I'll never 'bring home the gold' as a figure skater or
downhill
ski racer
(but who cares - I've always been more of a
summer person anyway)

my actions on the job, my work ethic
they don't exactly scream
'Upper Management'

(but that's o.k. - I'm kinda
uncomfortable
in a suit and tie)

can't play guitar and my
voice is shit,

this leads me to believe that the
'BIG TIME' music scene, may be out of my reach
(and that's alright too, 'cause
If I had all that
'BIG TIME' cash,
I'd be
'BIG TIME' dead, in about a month
(Note: this is only an estimate and if anyone is interested in
sending me some
'BIG TIME' cash just email mr.dempsey@hotmail.com and
we can work something out, maybe a 2 or
3 month clause)

hey,
I'm good with numbers
and science,
but I don't think
I'll invent anything nuclear or
sub
atomic (too much work in all that)

won't make CEO
of some wild start-up and I'm positive that NASA
doesn't want me either (but I'm DYING
to get off the earth for a while - You hear me NASA? -
DYING GODDAMNIT!)

so,
like I said earlier . . . woke up this morning (6 am, drank 2
beers in the shower while jacking off, smoked a roach that
was crawling in the ashtray) and
realized -

that I had better
learn to write

☙ DRAWING THE LINE

It's never enough for you, is it? You always want more. More beer, more sex.
More pills! Everything!

That's right honey.

But when are you gonna call it quits? When is it finally gonna be enough?

It'll never be enough.

And that's what scares me. You know, all you're doing is killing yourself.

Maybe.

And if you're not dead by 30, then you've got one hell of a shitty future to look forward to.

Maybe.

And you know you're doing it, but it doesn't matter, you just want more . . .

(It's true.)
There's never enough -
to drink,
to smoke,
never enough
good music
or
good art, never(!), never enough
laughter, or REAL people with REAL mouths and brains and insides,

(Plastic hearts! Vinyl souls! Assembly line organisms!
Nobody
is born with REAL guts anymore!)

never(!) and, (you might ask)
why?
Why do you see things like this?

Why do you always want more?
What are you pushing for? Where
do you think
this is all going to lead?

And I,
couldn't tell you - I honestly

don't know.

All

I'm sure of
is that I'm young and crazy and that should be enough
to get me by.

❧ A STEP ALONG THE WAY

an awkward kiss, my hands
all over her body while the heat
came down
around us - like an invading army
like a
young Hitler and we
tumbled
across her floor and onto
the bed . . .

it was like
all the magazine people
I had seen by flashlight; we
tangled arms and legs and
I don't think
I
'became a man'
that day - I think I just
understood
a little more

ℭℛ HOW DO YOU DO IT?

How do you do it? Simple

1) Fall in love with murderers
and believe every inch of their smiles.

2) Wake up in San Francisco, New Orleans, Barbados,
Manhattan
and check your license
to make sure of who you are.

3) Walk wide circles around religion
and believe only
in your hardcover heroes.

4) Drink this beer
like it's some life support system
and pay no attention
to the blood in your phlegm.

I've been taking these steps
without noticing the pattern. (it's only a dance - only a dance
John,
just keep moving your feet) And I'm willing to bet the
fucking farm on these theories.
In fact -

I'm willing to slug two quarts of gasoline and smile in some
dirty moonlight
while wiring electrodes to my jaw line to
prove
my
self
to
my-

self?

- Is that fucken pathetic?
Paste idiot heart
to this worthless page,

because I'm so

sure - (yeah it is, but keep pushing, don't let your foot off the
gas, show these guys
exactly what you're made of - and what am I made of?
Sludge and sewer drip, blood like an atom bomb, heavy
distortion on London radio and heavy buzz
through my beautiful brains - Vacancy - 25 Rooms with
Cable access -
that's the dempsey mind - 400 channels of . . . What? Of
everything. Flash scenes
of demented dreams
and run the flag
between the legs of an idol. Isn't that what we're after?
Sitting in a little room - "working on something good - but if
it's really good - you're gonna need a bigger room - and
when you're in the bigger room - you might not know what to
do - you might have to think of - how you got started - sitting
in your little room" - and that's borrowed, pulled from the
white stripes, because jack white
can write some fucking lyrics -

I'm

bleeding punk rock guitar
in some foreign café
and there's this gnawing in my gut -

tells me
that I'm not alone.

☙ DRIVE PAST THE SUN

look - shoot guns and drink Canadian beer, call your woman
at 3 in the morning and tell her you've designed the prototype
for a machine that allows you to traverse the anal time
continuum - you need her to come over - Right Now! - so that
she can help you test it.

man - buy coke and xanax, speed off on one and slow down

with the other, toss empty bottles from moving cars while listening to 80's punk, burning holes in the upholstery and dreaming of sail fish.

shit - get a job as a telemarketer then get fired for making prank phone calls, get a job as a landscaper then get fired for drinking in the tool shed, a fence painter and lose that one for giving the neighbor's dog
some
flare.

mother - roll outa bed at 6 and smoke 2 bowls of resin, play guitar for an hour, jerk off, shower, throw on a Cuban hat and an eye patch, stand naked at the window with your stomach pressed against the glass, eating an
egg
sandwich.

fuck - tape zucchini to your thigh and wear tight jeans, comb your hair, spray cologne and lean with your back to the bar, hips thrust out like some jet set playboy type in your nice
polo
shirt.

me? - I'm shadow boxing on a Friday morning, the bank account reads 17.50 and all I want to do
is

drive past the sun.

☙ GOOD COMPANY

She had been abroad, a broad, for something like 6 yrs traveling - Italy, Spain, Greece, Holland - and I'd get these postcards:

'John - I'm in (Italy, Spain, Greece, Holland) and I'm working as a (waitress, English teacher, bartender, call girl) and I want you to know that I'm thinking about you.'

Never a return address or a phone number, nothing,

and then
last night,
sitting on the couch - hand in my lap, cold beer, watching
triple x television - the phone started ringing:

"John, I'm in New York, out of work and hanging around the
Village. I still think about you."

And so I gave her an address,
found a pair of clean boxer shorts and played the waiting
game.

Some time later I heard a set of
high heels on the staircase - my dick stood up and told me to
open the door - I listened - (Always pay attention to the body!
If the body tells you to do something, anything, light fires or
punch policemen, then do it!) - and the broad from abroad
was there in a red dress and there was international sex
pumping heavy from her figure - she smiled and I smiled and
we hugged/kissed hello and there was this
5 gallon
box of white wine in the fridge and so I poured out a couple
of glasses.

"It's good to see you John. How long has it been?"

"Too long baby, too long. Remember all the crazy shit we
used to get into? Remember when we got caught on the roof
that one time and I kept saying that there was gravel in my
ass?"

"Of course I remember. How about when we drove out to the
beach in the middle of November and we sat under the
boardwalk drinking that rum punch you made."

"Yeah, yeah, that was a good time."

"Yeah it was."

"So how are you doing now? How's life on the move treating
you?"

"Oh, I like it and all, I'm meeting a lot of people and seeing a
lot of things, but, sometimes I just, I don't know, it's just, just
sometimes I feel so lonely, you know, lonely and crazy. Does

that make sense?"

"Shit honey, yeah it makes sense, we're all lonely and crazy.
Welcome to mother earth."

"You really think so?"

"Yeah, in our own way, we're all fucked up like that.
Everybody's scared and alone and nuts. Everybody!
Everywhere! And you know what, if by some
odd chance
I'm wrong and it's really just the two of us that are like this,
then, then . . .
then I'll get myself a gun and shoot big holes through
everyone who thinks differently. How's that for rationalism?"

"Haha, very rational John, very rational. You know, you
haven't changed a bit. Well, you look like you might've put
on a few pounds, but that's about it."

"Yeah, beer weight, I know."

"But you're still the same John, I knew it would help talking
to you."

And so we went to work on the box of wine and on our
clothes and eventually into bed with our lonely,
crazy selves
clinging and clutching at one another,
reaching out and holding on and for the first time, in a long
time,
we were both
happy
and sane and we didn't even
have to worry about
being lonely
anymore.

‍ℭ‍ℜ FINELY SKINNED CLOUDS

finely skinned clouds

Her mouth is strange
Her eyes are strange

Pan-fried sunshine
Winter recall
Laughed real fine while playing in the gutter
(embracing despair)

Floating head, cum/words drip off golden lips and the
windowpane slams on clumsy thumb

Clouds
Blue thinking
Dead thought
Frozen thought
Dead winter
Blue eyes
Brown body
She left for Miami and I sat on the corner of West 3rd,
pulling on burnt tobacco and thinking about her legs

Stray cats
Talking heads - 80's bar puke motif everybody drips fake
blood and cocaine flakes
snow down
real gentle

There are terms we'll never understand

Falling soft
King trumpets
(Floating-Floating-Floating)

The light doesn't sound too good
The reception aint comin in so clear

And mental instability
is just another term for freedom

Miniskirt catechism
and God (who's?) as my witness
I will stand by these 2 women
for at least a week
before I pick up a third - john

ＣＲ Don't Bet On The Women

In conversation with the Italian poet
we come to the conclusion:

That at first YOU control words, make them sit, beg, roll over
etc.
but the longer you play with them
you find that the words're the ones holding the leash
while you're out pissing on the sidewalk . . .

Mr. Henry,
I think we must add to that -

The women

they move like Monets
they move like bullet trains
they move live time itself and at first you can sit and study
that Monet
or you can buy that train ticket or you can play with the
minute hand on your watch,
but eventually,
they turn - you realize
that the painting is a knockoff
the train is headed for some dead city
where the mayor
is 'someone else, someone who really knows how to treat a
woman'
and the watch
is no more
than costume jewelry
with a dead battery . . .

What can you do with a fake Monet?
(nothing)
How do you jump off a train without getting hurt?
(you can't)
And what pawnshop is gonna buy a cheap watch?
(none)

So,
Mr. Henry
I've come to another conclusion:

Don't bet on the women,
they're the
longest shot
of all

ᏲᏋ GETTING ALONG

And my ears were heavy
with the sound of birds.

I sat outside (trees and sky) with lightning through my head,
thinking about a brunette
from

6 yrs ago -

always liked it from behind, had to eat her out first, too.

And I was playing some
Jane's Addiction song
on this
maple brown
vintage guitar -

Summer Time Rolls. That's the name of it, always made me
think of her.

And then I remembered: that brunette was nothing but a
whore.

Screw'er.

Now I'm inside (glass and walls) typing bad poems, thinking
about a painting
I saw just the other day - Cubism,
pure style, I'm a

fucking renaissance man . . .

In five minutes
the phone will ring.

It will be a man from East Desmoines,
he'll ask me if I'm interested in a Visa Gold Card and I'll ask
him
where he thinks my secret mole is:

"You get one chance, you slippery prick. Guess where my
secret mole is and I'll sign up for one of your cards."
"Ummm-ughhh . . . Is it on your thigh?"

It's on my shaft, I'll hang up the phone. Pinch my cheek.
Giggle. There's a mirror
right there so I can watch myself have a conversation.
It's real interesting -
try it sometime . . .

The clock reads happy hour. It tells me that people are out.
That people are doing things. That society is moving. And it
asks:
Why don't you move with it?
Answer: Because I'm a dropout and a headcase and I'd rather
sit here, in a dark room,
with the Russian novelists, than be out there
with the dead
goat
herd. Sorry,

but

there's Soul here.

There's LIFE here.

No

hair gel heavy cologne smile with the just whitened teeth and silk shirt open at the chest -

Sorry, there's

just

john.

⊂⊃ CONVERSATIONS WITH THE ITALIAN

(So I meet with the Italian
and we grapple with demons . . .)

The new shit is coming out too slow, he tells me, but I guess
you can't force the gods.

Nah man, they smile when they want - piss the rest of the
time.

Hey, how many poems have you written so far?

This year? I don't know, but I'm up in the 250-275 page
range. Maybe 100 poems in that, maybe more.

Hmm . . . there's a lot to edit there.

Yeah there is, and the problem is that once you write
something, and you're happy with it, you move on - going
back to edit is like fingering an ex girlfriend with a big pussy
- it just doesn't fit right anymore.

Hahahaha! (He takes a deep breath, then really lets it out)

HAHAHAHAHAHA!

It really is man; I'd rather beat off with my new poems than
screw the old lovers. Hey, you hear of this band called the
white stripes?

You already asked me that . . . still the same answer . . . NO!
I haven't.

Short term memory loss - my mistake.

80's punk kinda vibe, right?

Yeah garage rock, cracking voice type shit - real good.

(The Italian, 3600 miles away, uncorks a bottle of red.
I'm on the job,
all saliva and envy, downtown, Manhattan, counting quarters,
nickels and dimes.)

Speaking about music . . . there's a giant party all over town
tonight. Tomorrow is Queen's Day and tonight there's a lot of
LIVE music going on, a celebration type thing.

That's right, I remember you telling me about that. Tonight,
I'm counting out change to make happy hour.

Hehehe.

So, you gonna check out the party tonight?

No way man . . . too fucking cold outside . . . it's something
like
6C . . .

Holy shit - shouldn't it be getting warmer?

It was! Goddamnit! But now the frigging wind has turned and
all hell has broken loose. No point in going out to freeze my
balls off.

Same here - we went from 96 to 46 in 2 fucken days - either
apocalypse or, maybe,
somebody's got a weather machine.

Heehee . . . the weather machine would be a cool trick.

Yeah and they're trying to trigger the end of the world - first
they force the downfall of the church - some sorta electronic
stimulation beam, turns the average pastor into a rampant,
randy type goat, real horny all the time - then they fuck with
the weather, jumble up climates and forecasts - bring snow
storms to the desert - frozen camels! What's next?

Whatever it is, we will find out too late.

You're right - the shithouse will be gone and we'll be looking
around for toilet paper - brown under our fingernails.

I applaud the downfall of the Church! It's about fucking time!

2000 years of sheer nonsense!

Hey, fucken yahoo cut off my service - it says I have 3 new emails but I can't fucken log in.

Yahoo sucks. More than the Back Street Boys!

More than the Church!

We should bomb their asses!!

I wish we could man. Who's asses?

Yahoo - can't you concoct a nice, all eating, and devastating lil virus?

I don't know man - never tried.

Don't you know any nice lil hacker?

Nah, I can't communicate with those types.

Some super pimpled, over sexed, bespectacled 15-year-old fucking computer genius.

Honestly - with billy gates bed sheets and cum shots by the pillow - Finally! I just got in - those fuckers at yahoo assigned me the dumbest of all passwords - steelponies - how in the hell am I gonna remember that?

Steelponies? Sounds like a teenage country-punk band.

Haha - Ah Shit Thank God! Only 20 more minutes till the happy hour whistle blows.

. . . the happy hour whistle - one of the most desired sounds in the world.

Yeah it is, well, for the enlightened man anyway.

That . . . and a cumming pussy

Only problem with pussy, it drags trouble like some sorta tail - happy hour just sucks up your cash and your brain cells - but at least its honest about the scam right from the beginning.

Hey, that's good. Maybe we should write all this down, maybe we can work a poem out of it!

Ah, I don't know, its the same bullshit I spew all the time -
the woman has heard it a
million times over. I'm almost sick of saying it.

Well . . . FUCK the woman! I wanna read those lines!

Haha - thank you man, they'll come out when they're ready.
It's funny how you can't
control the words, it's like, all of a sudden they're holding the
leash while you're the one out pissing on the street - it really
is a game.

There you go again! Man!

Haha - my body knows that the hour is coming.

Do me a favor . . . read this conversation we're having . . .
there's gotta be something useful in it! How do you do it
man?

I don't know.

Talent.

Nah - not talent, just guts and dead brain cells - and anyone
can get that - just gotta put your money on the bar and your
balls on the line.

Whatever, just get to your happy hour.

Ah, my mouth is all water right now from those two little
words.

WATER TO THE PLANTS! WATER TO THE FLOWERS!
WE BREATHE LIQUIDS! WE THRIVE ON TOXICITY!
WE NEED, WE NEED . . . WE NEED HIGH OCTANE
ALCOHOL!

No way, man. I've been taking it easy ever since I smashed
that Mexican guitar in a fit of 151- now its beer and dewars
for a while. Damn toxic 151.

WE THRIVE ON TOXICITY!

I know, you're right. We need it! Ok - I'm gonna take off,
maybe we can get something nice and pretty out of all the
broken glass and abused condoms lying round here - diamond

in the trash heap sorta thing, but right now, the dewars is screaming from the bar shelf and I promised I'd be down there to keep him quiet.

Haha, ok man, make sure you have one on me - and thanx for the talk.

Same here - you just helped me get thru demon Monday

You know, of course, that tomorrow is demon Tuesday.

Ah fuck! One dirty step at a time, man - One dirty step at a time or else they'll cut us off at the knees.

But then again, we surf on the waves of repetition.

But for how long, that's the question

Ok, pilgrim . . . I'll talk to you later . . . gotta see a man about a dog . . . I'll probably end up kicking the dog, but . . .

Those fucken dogs! - Always biting!

Always!

And never letting go!

Never!

(And the Italian signs off,
and I walk out,
and the demons are kept at bay,
for a little while longer.)

☯ BIC-PEN GAMBLING

you're only as good as that last thing you wrote
(poem/story/hate-mail/what
ever it was that you dragged your ass out of bed to type)
and you're hoping that
THAT last thing
wasn't really THE last thing cause then you'd really be
screwed, this is one gamble where you bet HEAVY (real

HEAVY, laid it all down on the line like it was some
SURE THING even though you knew it was
THE LONG SHOT - you figured on bad aim from the firing
squad and honey,
they've turned out to be sharp shooters - what are
YOU
going to DO?) (idontknow-
drinkbeerandsmokefilteredRedsand
curseattheceilingtillifindsomesortasomethingtogetdownonthe
godamnedpaper - that soundsliketherightthingtobedoing -
ithink) so . . . about that HEAVY bet you laid down . . . you
can't lose this one, you're going to have to pay in blood and
mind and future, this has stopped being
the
HEAVY bet-
it's become tidal wave lifestyle and self destructive mentality;
jumping on that
one-way plane for Kamikaze run,
destination un
       known and that's A-
O-K
as far as
you
   're
con
   cerned-

Now - for (post card pretty religion fervor hallmark fantasy
type artists)
GREEN
boys and girls out there, itching
for a literary name
up in
literary lights,
just
remember:
one way trip, really is
      1 Way Trip; no
        return
and

one step
off the ledge of MEDIOCRE
really is
          a

ten
     story
          drop

CR DEAR SIR

I got off the downtown C: 7 am, nicotined, caffeinated tetra-
hydrocannabinolated, and saw this short one; no more than
110 pounds
blonde hair and the gray, above the knee, business skirt, no
stockings, pink rimmed
glasses and pink curved
lips - her body language yelling NEED - NEED - I
NEED (5 sweaty hours, with you, johnjohn -
legs wrapped and mouth open, eyes shut and
internal
explosion
shaking
the walls) - I followed that body 9 blocks Sir, skirt and mad
bouncing ass, golden legs dancing on Manhattan sidewalk,
she smelled good too, clean, like -
that first day of summer smell and the wind was just right,
blowing all that clean summer towards my nose and I closed
my eyes, inhaled real deep, held it and when I opened back
up -

She was gone, disappeared through some black hole in space

I turned back, heading for the office, still early, only 8 or so
and the street was already heavy: (so-called people): all types
of them, lugging dogfaces and
kangaroo pouches, some even had these little alligator
children with muzzles fitted round their snouts, they walked
them on leashes and the fashion was metal spiked collars -

one small gator child, stood apart from the rest;
she sported pink eyes and
white marble skin.

An albino! I started to follow and next thing I know Sir:

Flash back to New Orleans:
holding hands with this voodoo woman, black magic and
absinthe in the morning,
remembering the aquarium, how I waited for the sharks to
swim up close, against the walls of the tank and I would snap
pictures of their eyes, bright FLASH-FLASH trying to get
some action out of them - not even a twitch, large, boring fish
and after 15 attempts we said 'Screw the Aquarium!' -
Walking out of the place, feeling ripped off by the site of lazy
octopi in their ridiculous tanks, tree frogs that didn't jump
like frogs and weren't even in trees, stuffed parrots with
mechanized loud speaker cawing . . .
All of it a rip off, and I told her:

'This place is the shits baby, same old scene as everywhere
else. Everything claims to BE something, claims to DO
something and it never measures up. Same tired janitor
pushing a dirty mop across the floor.' and we work towards
the exit where we notice a crowd around this one area, there
attention fixed on something and we want to see that
something too, we push for the front, get to the edge of the
tank and
Holy Shit!

One of the wildest things I've ever seen:
An albino alligator, bigger than DEATH, white scales and
pink killer eyes, some NO-FEAR type walks around the gator
like it's a housecat, talks into a wireless microphone ' . . . the
only one in captivity. Diet consists mostly of . . . ' he throws
scraps of meat from a potato sack and I'm thinking:

What happens when he runs outa those scraps? And this
thought flashes me forward; I look towards the gator child
I'm following, wondering about scraps and muzzles and
holding tanks. I shake off New Orleans and when the gator
child is brought to a building

· 24 ·

(a plaque above the door reads: Le-Bryant School for the Gifted) I walk past, there's music coming from a cab stopped at the traffic signal on my left, and the song, well, it just sorta sucked me in Sir:

'2 weeks in the Virginia jail
For my lover, for my lover
20,000-dollar bail
For my lover, for my lover . . . '

And this brings me to that one summer in Syracuse, 4 in the morning with a deadly brunette, snorting white lines off a naked hipbone, tongue flicks at the small trace of powder and she moans, heavy with anticipation and we made it slow while her sister slept in the next room, that song was playing . . . for my lover, for my lover . . . I'd say it in her ear as we rocked. It was magic Sir, real life, true shit magic and I remember how she killed me, just a little bit that summer, and how it made me stronger cause I walked towards that death like it was no big thing, stepped into the coffin, smiling up
into her wet eyes . . . (drip-drip of tears on silk casket lining) and when I was reborn her image had been blasted from my memory, I came up outa the ground like some under dog in a title match, a prize fighter who took no prisoners, shooting first and saying screw the questions.

I saw her, once more, on the street. Her still wet eyes meant nothing to me Sir, you understand, I had grown a protective like shell and I shot death/hate-stare at her, full blast, max power, and she crumbled like sugar cubes in hot water and that made me feel good so I smiled that same coffin-smile.

Then the light changed to green, the cab took off and I decided on making the office. It couldn't have been more then 10 o'clock by then and I was maybe 18 blocks from the job. I pointed myself in the direction of (slow-idiot-corporate-torture-death) the office and told myself no more daydreaming, no more stalking of albino gator children or past life reminiscing, straight ahead, one step after another till I hit the 9 2 5.

I made ten blocks real easy, smoking a cigarette and undressing women with my imagination. As you know Sir, the city is rampant with these creatures. Breasts and legs and smiles, tight skin holding in guts and muscle and blood (and I'm sure that somewhere in all that mess is a heart). This one in particular must've been close to 7 feet tall. All that flesh and sex, wobbling in high heels down West Fourth, a giant; each breast must've weighed 30 pounds and her legs were long, long, long! They led up to this large, magnificent ass, and that ass Sir, why, it was just plain insanity to stare at, those round cheeks moving to some intrinsic sex beat that had been programmed into her giant thoughts, and I was hypnotized; I walked and drooled my way to the building Sir. I saw the doors, the I.D. checking security guard, the bank of elevators that stood waiting to zip me up to the office, but as I walked past, all that large, glorious ass on my mind, I didn't have time for rational thought, I kept following with pervert spittle hanging off my lip. I followed her to Christopher Street and onto the 1/9 downtown local, making stops at Houston, Canal and Franklin. At Franklin she pulled a book from her purse and started reading. I saw the book jacket and read the title: Journey to Ixtalan, Mr. Castenada, and I've read that work Sir. Some serious words in that but I'll tell you what, I found that the lessons were basically impossible to follow given the current century and my geographic location, but the look on that giant woman's face, she was absorbed in it, hooked on every word, I could picture the gears in her head working, she was thinking of plane tickets and relocation, of picking up these words and living her life by them and Sir, that just simply turned me off.

Here was another creature hell bent on somebody else's life and only hoping to follow in footsteps instead of laying down fresh tracks. So at Franklin I jumped off that damned 1/9 local. I ran up the platform and saw a clock. The clock said 11:15 and I knew I was late, but I thought that if I really moved, caught the A uptown express and hauled ass past the park, I'd make it in before lunch.

Well Sir, that plan didn't execute itself

as smoothly as I had hoped.

I made the corner of Hudson and I remembered this one bar where I would meet up with The European and drink heavy on Thursday nights. That was last year but I was curious and so I went a couple blocks out of the way to check it out. The place was still the same - Fritz, the owner; served imported, draft beer at a machine gun pace. The power lunch crowd infested the bar, screaming drink orders and talking office politics. I got wrapped right up in the scene. Sat down next to a couple of suits and yelled down the line:

Dewars and Coke!

By 1 the lunch crowd was gone and I sat there talking with Fritz. He's really a good guy Sir, quite the philosopher and the drinks kept coming, I wasn't ordering, they just came, real automatic like and I'm not one for insulting the generosity of others, you know?

I played the decent guy role and sucked that liquid right up into my silly little brains.

Then Fritz looked at his wristwatch and said '2:30 - already?' and I peeled my ass off that barstool - lightening fast. Said my good bye and bolted through the door.

Sir, I was feeling good. (booze)
But I was also feeling bad. (unreliable)
Mixed emotions on a Monday afternoon and I told myself:

'Just get to the office johnny boy, say you got into some wild shit, some accident and that you'll make it up, stay late and work some midnight shift, apologize if you have to.'

So I worked out a story in my head. I was gonna tell you that there was a fire in my apartment building and that after everybody was evacuated I saw this white cat in one of the windows. The cat was trapped, meowing and there was smoke behind it. I was gonna tell you that I'm an animal lover and that I couldn't stand by while that helpless little kitten burned real painful like and the firemen were standing round scratching at balls and looking disinterested so I rushed back up the stairs, choking on smoke and eyes burning. I was gonna tell you that I could hear the cat behind this one door. That there was smoke curling up from under the frame and I was just real tough about the whole thing, real manly and all, and just delivered this serious kick to the door, knocking it shit from hinges across the apartment and that this little white kitten was half dead, stumbling round the place when I came in, but with its last drop of energy, it's life-drive it jumped into my arms and I nestled my face into it's fur, kissed it gentle and whispered:

'It's o.k. baby kitten. You're all safe now and snuggled in my armor.'

Then I was gonna tell you that I rushed back out the building and onto the street, that all the building tenants were cooing and oh my godding and what a hero in my ear, and me being dressed for the job just brushed past all that, dropped off the kitten to a crying woman and made the train. Then I realized that you probably watch television. And I know that on television is this program called The News. The News would tell you if something like that had happened and once you saw that it didn't, you'd say:

'Why, that lying scum!'

and then I'd be out of a job, and that would be o.k. if I didn't have so many monkeys to look after, but Sir, I have an awful lot of monkeys. New ones pop up on my back like acne and grab hold, sinking sharp teeth and digging dagger claws. Now Sir, I don't know what your experience with monkeys is and so I'll let you in on a little 'insider' information.

Monkeys will never take no for an answer.

It's that simple Sir, and I am somewhat unsure of why I wrote you this letter but I think I can sum it up:

Sorry I didn't make it in today, there were some, uh, unexpected occurrences on my commute - completely out of my hands - and I would've called you nice and early this morning but LIFE
travels faster than light and I'm a slow, slow mover at times. Hope all is well in the office and I'll see you tomorrow - john

✆ A.C. With The Giant

We, the Giant and myself, pulled into Atlantic City at 11 pm in a white van and the sky was all flashing lights and neon bulbs and bright fireworks shooting across the horizon.

12 hrs earlier -

We had taken 16 ounces out of an apartment on the Upper West side in exchange for a thousand dollars cash.

24 hrs earlier -

We were hustling around the East Village, leaning on contacts - this is how it worked:

Line up 7 guys who'll pay a buck 50 each for 28 grams of decent green. That gives us
(7 X 150)
10 fifty for capital and that covers the 16 ounces, of which we owe out seven and leaves us with 9 ounces of free bud and 50 dollars in profit - it's not a bad little scheme.

We distribute the seven, dump another 5, at the same price (5 X 150(+ 50), 800 tax free dollars and four ounces and we sat at an uptown bar, drinking expensive drinks with red eyes and full pockets and an idea flashed through my head and I jumped off the stool and yelled: lets make the tables!

It was early afternoon and we got outa the bar. Walked 3 blocks to the barber. He shaved our faces with a hot blade and then cut our hair. Then we walked 5 blocks to a shop that had mannequins in pinstripe suits and colorful ties standing in the window. 2 hours later we had been fitted for suits, shirts, ties and shoes and we hit the street with boxes and bags and we even took showers and sprayed Japanese cologne across our hairless necks and the mirror told us that we were a couple of good looking fuckers and we still had 400 bucks and lots of smoke and so we rolled 4 big joints, bought two 6 packs, of imported beer, got into the white van, gassed up and started heading south.

We drove three and a half hours, smoked 3 joints and (once again) we, the Giant and myself, pulled into Atlantic City at 11 pm and the sky was all flashing lights and neon bulbs and bright fireworks shooting colored sparks across the horizon and we paid two dollars to park at Caesar's Casino. We sat in the van working on the imported beer and reading a blackjack strategy chart that told us when to hit, stand, split and double down based on multi deck probabilities and we must've sat in that white van for close to two hours in our shiny clothes and trimmed hair, drinking the beer and memorizing the rules and smoking filtered cigarettes till we had finished the beer and when we stepped outa the van, in a cloud of smoke, we looked good and we felt like winners and there was big money dreams turning cartwheels through our thoughts: we were going to break the bank! Shit - we were going to beat the house; it was in the air and it was in our blood and it was everywhere, it was in every body, every face we passed held that same expression - tonight was for gambling. And not just gambling - but gambling and winning. Winning! Shit! That's the key. Any degenerate can put chips on a table and yell hit, stand, split or double down, but it takes a certain something, a certain feel for the cards and a respect for the house in order to walk away a winner.

Strutting down the casino floor we pass by a wall of mirrors, I take a quick glance at our reflection, and I see winners. Tonight was it. We were gonna make it.

It took 20 minutes to find a table with a minimum bet of 15 dollars and we both got seats. I secured the anchor position and the Giant sat two chairs to my right. In our fresh suits and crisp shirts we laid out 200 bucks in twenty dollar bills and the first hand was a dealer's bust and that was a good way to start since we both bet double the minimum and that's a net gain of 60 bucks in about 30 seconds. Fantastic! Balls of goddamned Fire! And that's how the night started. We played that table for a little over 3 hours. I watched the Giant and he watched me and we helped each other out with head nods and headshakes and by the time we decided on taking a break I estimated that our value was up around 700 bucks.

We cashed out and hit the casino bar. I ordered DewarsandCokewithalime and the Giant was on SevenandSeven. We bought two cigars each, for 6 dollars a pop, bit off the ends, and lit up.

The Giant: 'Not a bad cigar.'
Me: 'Nah, not at all.'
Giant: 'I like the feel of this place. It feels lucky.'
Me: 'Yeah, we're doing pretty good here. I think we should stick to this casino.'
G: 'Definitely. Lets have a couple more drinks then what do you say about giving the Roulette wheel a shot?'
Me: 'I can do that.'

We had a couple more, tipped the bartender with a ten, and headed for the Roulette table. 50 bucks red! The little ball stops on 26. That's black. Mother! Another 50 on red and we get lucky with a seven. Once more, 32 comes up and that's red and we puff on the 6-dollar cigars and everything sparkles and nothing is impossible when you're betting with easy made money and winning. Nothing. And so we push our luck and come up with another hundred dollars and head back to the bar to cool off. ("And why would you want to cool off?" you ask. "Because, it allows you to stick to one of the most important rules of gambling." "Which is?" "Never place a bet based on your emotions.

You needed to stay calm. The gambling bug bites fast and once those teeth get a hold, the frenzy begins. That's what you need to avoid.") The bartender remembered us and came around with the drinks without us having to order and I liked that.

The Giant: 'Hey how much you think we've made so far?
Me: 'It's gotta be close to 800 bucks. We're fucken champs tonight!'
The Giant: 'Let's hope it lasts. I say we work for the thousand-dollar mark, and if we make that, we should get a room for the night, see if maybe there's any women around.'

And vultures
can smell a dying animal

before the animal
even knows that it's dying.

They've got a great sense of smell. Apparently, they also
have good ears because those words fell out of the Giant's
mouth, floated through the casino air, and were picked up by
two brunettes in high heels and long hair and they sat two
stools down the bar from us and kept looking over with screw
me smiles and heavy cleavage and I could feel my dick,
trying to control my mind and so I used this special trick in
order to stay focused. It's real simple. First think about what
it would be like to screw one of them, very nice, and then
think about the morning after and the 'hey, I gotta start
heading home' awkward as all hell conversation with
hangover brain and ashtray mouth and it works for me almost
every time, almost, and so it was back to the tables. We both
had that second cigar sticking out of our faces and walking
back to the cards
we left blue smoke
in our wake
and that was more than enough
of a trail
for the vultures to follow.

It was closing in on 5 am, the booze ran through my system
and dulled my senses and sleep deprivation and those joints
and the cigars and I started making bad decisions at the table
and lost 100 bucks in about 10 minutes. The Giant was still
on his game, in the zone, and he sucked up that hundred, plus
another 60, and my fingers were shaky so I got up and let him
handle the cards while I sucked on beer. The vultures took
note of my condition. They flew patterns around the table and
smiled pretty and my mind trick stopped working because I
got to thinking about screwing the both of them at the same
time and to hell with the morning after.

I stopped watching the Giant when one of the vultures landed
next to me and opened her beak.

Vulture: 'Excuse me, do you have a match?'
Me: 'Here you go.'

Vulture: 'Thanks.'
Me: 'No problem.'
Vulture: 'How come you aren't playing?'
Me: 'Ah, I think my luck is done for tonight.'
Vulture: 'Don't be so sure, you've still got a chance.'
Me: 'Oh yeah, and how do you figure that?
Vulture: 'Well, I'm here.'
Me: 'Oh.'
Vulture: 'Yeah'
Me: 'Hmmm . . . ' and then I called over my shoulder 'Hey, Giant, you wanna get outa here?'

And there was no answer so I looked over to where I last saw him and see a pile of chips and a smiling giant and that second vulture was perched oh so pretty in his big old lap.

We cashed in, left the casino and went to a place, called simply, 'The Irish Pub'. There, we drank tap beer from big mugs while the vultures chirped around some aqua blue drink, electriclemonade, and they pressed legs and breasts up against us and we called for shots and we felt like big shots with our nice suits and stuffed pockets and we called for even more shots and then more shots and next I know a phone was ringing and I was

on the floor

of some place

I had never seen before and my head was spinning like I had just gotten off some cocaine-crazed carousal that rotated at a thousand rpm's and I wasn't wearing the pinstripe suit anymore. I was in fish print boxers and the Giant snored heavy and loud and he was in boxers with fire engines on them and the phone wasn't waking him up so I answered and an operator told me:

Operator: 'Good morning Mr. Dempsey, I just wanted to remind you that check out time is 11 am.'
Me: 'Check out time? Shit, where am I?'
Operator: 'You're in suite 211 of the Sands Hotel.'
Me: 'Oh . . . fuck what happened last night?

Operator: 'I'm not sure sir.'

Me: 'Oh . . . ok, thanks, we'll get our shit together and be down in a little bit.'

Operator: 'Well you have an hour before room service comes to make up the room.'

Me: 'Alright, thanks.'

I decided on a shower. When I got out the Giant was on all fours with his head under the bed frame. (Reading this over I decide that that line is rather gay, but fuck it, no changes, no edits, just typing.)

Me: 'Hey, what are you doing?'

The Giant: 'Looking for our money, for our clothes, anything! I think those whores cleaned us out.'

Me: 'Yeah they did.'

The Giant: 'Did we at least get laid.'

Me: 'I don't think so.'

The Giant: 'Fuck!'

Me: 'Yeah, I know man, I know.'

The Giant: 'What are we gonna do? All that cash - FUCK - I swear to god I'm gonna kill those whores!'

Me: 'C'mon, get your shit together, we still have to check out.'

The Giant: 'What shit? They took everything we had. And how the hell are we gonna check out? How did we even check in?'

Me: 'I have no idea. Lets just try and make the van. You got a spare key?'

The Giant: 'Yeah, hidden in the dash.'

Me: 'Ok, lets take the stairs.'

We hurried down two flights, came to a door marked fire exit, opened it, and an alarm went off. We started running. Made the boardwalk. Boxer shorts with sail fish and fire engines and the morning crowd looking at us and the scene was funny so I started laughing but the Giant wasn't amused and he was cursing

fucking

vulture

whores all the way back to Caesar's and when we pushed

through the glass doors, two guards were on us in 5 seconds. We were manhandled, then escorted to the parking garage and I was still laughing but they called for backup and it took three guards to manhandle and escort the Giant.

We got to the van. The Giant put his elbow through the back window, gave me a boost, and I slithered all snake like and cut my belly on some glass, opened the door, found the spare, still had a joint and so we lit that, pulled out of Caesar's and started heading north. I took a few pulls
and closed my eyes . . .

Woke up on the BQE (Brooklyn-Queens Expressway) and threw a cigarette into my mouth, smoked that, yawned and 20 minutes later, we, the Giant and myself, dressed only in boxer shorts, pulled into Manhattan in a white van and the skyline was all tall buildings and gray-black storm clouds floating real easy across the horizon.

Less than 12 hrs earlier -

We had been taken for close to 1100 bucks and two pinstripe suits by some whores in Atlantic City and I guess they must've slipped some kind of pills into our drinks when we weren't paying attention.

We made the apartment and still had lots of bud left so we rolled a couple of joints, lit up and thought about how we were gonna line up another 7 guys who'll pay a buck 50 each for 28 grams of decent green and that would gives us
(7 X 150)
10 fifty for capital and that covers the 16 ounces, of which we owe out seven and leaves us with 9 ounces of free bud and 50 dollars in profit. We got dressed, hustled down to the East Village, and started leaning on our contacts.

CR A SERIOUS ARTIST

Type poems while jacking off?
Me?
No,
I'd never do that, that's simply disgusting, down right
disturbing!
at 8fourteen
with one hand
on the keyboard....

       I'm in a bubble, somewhere in the middle of the
ocean and there's
      a master switch
         that reads OFF.

The mind has gone to complete jelly.
There are spiders,
that crawl my pant's leg with red lust abandon, eight legs
and two fangs,
bug eyes
staring . . .

       And I'm in a bubble, somewhere in the middle of
the ocean
      and there's a bloated body
         beginning to reek.

15 blow up dolls, they can't be wrong - "John
you look so good,
with 4 teeth missing."
Sunburn down the front of my body
while the back
is bone white . . .

       And I'm in a bubble, somewhere in the middle of
the ocean and
      there's an old saying
         about dead men
    and all the tales
that they tell . . .

Well I'm just sitting here, smiling real pretty for the cameras,
and I'll just leave this up to you,
about typing poems
while jacking off,
what do you think . . .

CR ON DEATH

death

comes without knocking
rides in and grabs hold
moving
steady - death grin
oozing

on horseback and by carrier pigeon
echoing
through hospital hallway and down
midnight alley - death hand
extended

written on cheap leaflets and distributed
to the literate
packaged by large corporations and sold
to a million
idol
dreamers - death grip
tightening

and Ernest
wrote it
with authority
then walked towards it
without
hesitation

I
watch it from the corner of my eye
10 stories

above midtown Manhattan
and I take a step
back
from that ledge - death touch
fading

I'm no
Ernest

❧ A MORNING PERSON

They come like clockwork; these
scheduled
explosions

They streak across the horizon; these
inevitable
mornings

the
'Where am I?' mornings -
an unfamiliar bed,
an alien bedroom,
some
back water
town (I can handle these types)

the 'Who am I?'
mornings -
the mirror screaming "STRANGER!
Those aren't your eyes!
There's no
LIFE
in them! - There's no
SOUL -
NO . . .
NO . . .
NOTHING,
NOTHING AT ALL!" (and these are

tough, but
manageable)

the
'Wait a minute,
what's your name again?' mornings - where
the straddling woman
becomes
the bucking nightmare (Fun!
Fun! Try
holding on
till you
get off)

and don't forget the
emergency
room mornings
or
the
downtown subway
mornings

There's also the
'Holy shit!
I'm on the beach!" mornings
and
the
'Holy shit!
Who put this dress on me?' mornings
(These are the roughest - maybe even worse than the
central booking-handcuffed to a desk-bleeding on the floor-
ripped clothes-zero
recollection and this black dude is lookin at me with wedding
night eyes at 7 in the . . . well,
maybe not
worse
than those)

I've always been a
morning person - all those
scheduled explosions,

those
inevitable
mornings, they're all just
so
perfect

❧ Q AND A

when this one calls
and asks me: john,
what are you up to? Wanna come over - do a couple bong hits
with
rubbing alcohol?

I can only answer:
Why not -

and when this one on the street asks: john,
what are you doing tonight? Wanna come by - drink beer on
my roof and feed
alka-seltzer to the pigeons

I can only answer:
Why not -

then there's this one in the mirror and when he asks: john,
what
are you doing with your life? Why
do you live like this? Why
do you write like this?

I can only answer:
Why not -

but when she asked me: john,
do you know how to love? Can I show you
how to love?

the only thing I could say was:
I'm not sure

CR LETCH

spent Thursday night
sweating
with a long-haired blonde on a long island
beach

told myself - this is it, all you need to be happy
is this
one woman

Friday night
moaning
tied to a headboard in jersey with a head case
named Heidi

told myself - maybe this is it, maybe all you need to be happy
are these
two
women

Saturday found me with an ex-girlfriend, 2 grams of coke
and a hard on

told myself - now you've done it, three women in
three days - you've just dug yourself
three
graves

on Sunday
the blonde came by the apartment, didn't knock, just walked
in the place
the ex was sleeping in the bedroom and I
was naked, drinking warm beer
in the kitchen -
Heidi was on the phone, breathing heavy and talking
handcuffs -
and I was lucky; saw the blonde
before she saw me - and ducked!
behind the counter as she moved towards the bedroom -
"John, Oh Johnny Boy" -

just loud enough
for Heidi to hear -
Heidi starts screaming and I hang up the phone -
long hair makes the bedroom, sees the ex and now she's
screaming and I
spot a pair of shorts on the floor - throw them on just as the
ex wakes up - now she's
screaming and I
bolt for the door,
run
down 5 blocks
in fish print
boxers
jump
into the 28 year old
marketing exec's window (she's another ex - got some of my
clothes in her closet) - get dressed, drink
2 coronas
from her fridge, take about 7 dollars
in quarters
and buy myself
some breakfast -

on Monday
went back to the apartment - coffee table
overturned, bathroom mirror
cracked and a
Dear Prick
letter on the counter - read the letter,
masturbated
and wrote
two poems-
this was one of them

☙ It's Just Not Happening Tonight

It's just not happening tonight -

The white rum tastes like rubbing alcohol (believe me,
I know - 5 glasses into the bottle)
This weed I picked up is real dry (might have been good at
one point,
but now it burns too fast - after 3 bowls)
I go outside - it' s too hot, spiders
crawl into my glass
wind up in my mouth - and that reminds me...

Maybe 7 yrs ago, this one, I called her Shelly,
short brown,
heavy drinker
with a bisexual
orientation,
had to
convince her to shave

(it took allot of dick.)

and this one time
we were in this other girl's garage - I called her Oki - don't
ask me why - and I caught this spider,
a real big fucker with a dark body and these green eyes and I
just tossed him into my mouth and grabbed a handful of
Shelly, back of the neck and pulled her in close, and she saw
the whole thing,
opened her mouth, sealed her
red lips around my own, and our tongues met somewhere in
the middle and the spider crawled,
back
and forth
from my mouth
into hers
and vice versa and we started getting hot and so I pulled
down her pants, reached my hand
down under her . . . No,

no, no - wait,
wait, sorry - I don't want to get side tracked with some stand
up sex scene - even if it was unbelievable - the way I turned
her around, pants down, panties, my right hand up her shirt,
hard nipples while my left hand, bent her over at the hip,
my pants,
already at the ankles, cock, jumping from the hole in my
shorts and soaking wet
Shelly as I got it in and her breathing and the sound she
makes when I start
to

slowly

grind . . .

See what I mean?

I don't want to get sidetracked - I was talking about the spider
and about how at that moment, when she opened her mouth
and took it all in,
me,
and the spider
and the scene
and the feeling
in the way we kissed each other, like,
it was the only moment
that mattered in our lives - just that instant
and nothing else and
when we pulled away
that first time,
and we looked at each other, no, into each other and we saw
something, something too big
to understand, something
beyond us
and our
comprehension I,
I,
I . . . wound up kissing her friend, she was a
long brunette
from South Africa, we were up against the fridge and she had

these legs that made my dick twitch and Aaaghhh . . . FUCK!

I'm -

Nowhere -

Fast -

all these pussy thoughts
won't
lay down
the
word for me tonight,

too many demons
playing jump rope in my head, all these faces
swim up from the memory, oh

momma,

nothing
seems to wanna work tonight, this whole thing is disjointed,
too many different (idiot, you're an idiot john) styles, too
much gamble - oh

baby, (she says to me)

don't u worry bouta thing, momma's here to make it alright -
I'm

just some young fuck,

there's more beer than there is me,
but I plan on changing that,

there's more weed than there is me,
but,
I plan on changing that too, and right now
im sitting here
in some green shirt,
and im tryin to figure out
how in the fuck
I can change you.

‍☙ Menial Task Enlightenment

- I polish screws and realize:
that
being born human
is a
learning
disability
in
and
of
it's
self

‍☙ Longaciddrive

The roads coil
stubborn head and back bent, big
black pupils -

I execute these complex motions - takes only
4 percent
of my attention.

These people all shift
their personalities
laugh
at my colored stomach and my tongue
feels
too big
for my own mouth.

By sunrise I'm drained, I'm asking:

Where do all the miles go? What do they lead to?
Is there
a
final destination? Anywhere? I

just

don't know - The roads

just
coil - These people

all shift - The answers

are a mystery and by sunrise
I'm

dead

sober.

○ゑ MARKETPLACE REVELATION

Underneath
the
greasy lights of theology
lie
soft schemes,
business plans
and
business attire - official
looking men
spew
absurd edicts and some people
are
actually
impressed - Cathlaholics.

I
weigh my religion as if it were fruit;
make sure I'm not getting ripped off, overcharged for rotten
crop, and I've checked out
a dozen
different vendors, but I
haven't found a
good deal

as of yet.

Beware
of these
short-change artists, they want
only
your soul.

CR IT's ALL RELATIVE

what is it? thursday? well,
then
it's thursday morning beer/rum shits - the hangover
humming
through the space between my ears - vision cloudy and the
mind
doesn't
want to respond in it's usual manner-
balance is off - hold on to the handrails - stairs makes me
nauseous -

ashtray

taste

mouth and abused face - chew five aspirin - large
iced coffee - pay with the trembling dollar (did I just make an
economic statement?) - 83 degrees, bright sun
and my love like a groundhog - freedom like a dark room -
sharks
swim through New York blacktop -
designer suits,
tailored around manicured fins - their stares
make me nauseous and yet
I feel
that
I'm
better.

❦ MID AFTERNOON IDENTITY CRISIS

3oh3
pm, time steps heavy and the calendar reads:

September 9th

awake on the floor, blood runs from the right nostril, spinning
head, no license, no credit cards,
I'm writing under John Dempsey and there's nothing to tell
me

that I'm anybody else (has it always been like this?)

(I can't remember) (well,
are you at least trying to remember?)
(I'm not so sure that I want to) (oh) (oh)
(yeah)

three17 with no chance of a miracle

will any of this amount to anything? awake on the floor,
scratched hands and darkened eyes

signs of a struggle and I'm the only one here, this doesn't
surprise me

everything in it's right place (but where is your right place) (I
don't know, is there such a thing?) (I highly doubt it, just
keep moving john, you'll get to where you gotta go) (oh) (oh)
(yeah)

3 twenty and I'm a missing person
back of the milk carton might as well be a mirror

Have you seen this child? Last spotted on August 24th,
outside of Delaware traveling in a black pickup truck. If you
have any information please call 1-800 . . .

and I placed that ad, and I bought out that 800 number and if
you have any idea, any clue as to
where I am,
just
drop a line

ᑕᗧ JIMMY AND NOWHERE AND THE ESCAPE DREAM

The 'Escape Dream' is to build some kinda buccaneering, goddamned psychedelic crazy, outfitted with hammocks and blondes type barge and the whole floating, jittering, drinking with pills messiness on international waters with the typewriter bouncing, pounding, leaving indents on the table and all I'm wearing is this black felt cloak and red lycra thong, handkerchief, tied-off at the neck, gunslinger, wild west shooter style with rusty pistols pointed up at the stars and the blue flame sparks fly goddamned sickly powerful as I pull both triggers and blast holes through the hydro-atomic-nuclear-anal missile alarm of 6 am.

'Operating at full capacity Sir, 1500 Killa-Johns and holding steady.'
(Killa-What's? I ask.)

And that's the sound of the engineer. He starts the morning workaday machine and that thing is designed specially and specifically to tar and feather, whack, smack, beat hell and piss out of our shitlessly shiftless and mundane faces. And the Sir is the perpetual Sir of paycheck addiction and real world ties and the supermarket shopping lines with ass dragging cashier and overhead the speakers blare price check, price check and the perpetual Sir comes over with big knowing stomach and bustling fat wealth of jiggling titties with the veins popping and bursting and flaring in ridiculous road map lines across the nose and the Sir says 2.49 Jimmy, get with the program Jimmy, third time this week you've asked me the same thing and the perpetual Sir is tired of these craw daddy questions Jimmy - got that Jimmy? Jimmy? And Jimmy is fed up. Dope tired from pleasure-life-excitement-freedom withdrawal and he's got that damned stoned look in his eyes again and turns on these liquid heels, like, allofasudden he's got this new backbone and its been built outa titanium rods and cobwebs get disturbed when Jimmy opens his mouth, been a long time, you understand, but he turns to the

perpetual Sir and tells him, lets him know, real softly, almost
soothingly, what he can do. (Jimmy) Go fuck yourself.
(Heroic Jimmy) Go fuck yourself and your 2.49 and fuck
your striped ties and dressy shoes and fuck your chubby wife
with the thick ankles and her amethyst earrings. Fuck this and
fuck that 'cause Jimmy's got life on the outside and this
shitbox glass and metal container with the three little air holes
and two blades of grass just
aint
cuttin it
no more daddy-o and so Jimmy vaults the register state pen
wall and kicks over a bag of charcoal and dances all ginger
and merry towards the sliding doors - so long Charley The
Bag Boy and Lenny The Meat Guy, so long Jenny The
Customer Service Girl with the long hair and big nipples, so
long fuckers, so long - and the doors swoosh and the doors
swish and they open right up and Jimmy dances through,
grinning and jigging something glorious and that Jimmy is
the freest mother on this side of planet Life. (Heroic Fucken
Jimmy!)

'Last train to Nowhere - now boarding.'

(And that's the sound of the 'Escape Dream', tooting and
whistling down the tracks to Nowhere.)

Big Booming Voice of the Conductor: "Disappear into the
iridescent, milky depths of invisibility and hassle free
breathing. A place (Nowhere) where the 9 to 5 is understood
as fool's gold and every man an island. A place where there's
silky little women with nice pretty insides just itching and
wiggling in their cotton panty seats, just waiting, to make a
man smile. Step right up fuckers, babes and bums, Johns and
Jakes and Janes alike! You're all welcome (Nowhere). We're
headed towards the god blasted Future (Nowhere). We're
gonna puncture the mesh of space-time and eat high octane
acid and jackhammer our way out of the Stock-Fucken-Life
(Nowhere). Have you ever dreamt of TOTAL freedom, well,
that dream can now be realized, but where you ask?
(Nowhere) All aboard babies, we're set for our final
departure (Nowhere)."

Heroic Fucken Jimmy half runs half dances up to the station platform with free spirit grin and screw the world outlook shining off his round moon conqueror's face.

Hey there, Mr. Conductor, is it too late to buy a ticket?
Not at all my good man, not at all. Hey, hold on a minute...
Aren't you (and the eyes get all blood filled and bleeding over with respect and admiration) Heroic Fucken Jimmy?
Yeah, I guess you could call me that.
Well, partner, if it weren't for you there wouldn't be a Nowhere. You're mind is the Nowhere-Mind! You've discovered the Nowhere-Plane! Shit! A goddamned pioneer is what you are, and seeing as how that's the case, YOU are your own ticket. Hop on hero! We're gonna pull outa this shit sucking stratosphere and paint the cosmos with sticky white jizz and jazz and horns and drum beats! Nowhere! All aboard fuckers! Nowhere! All aboard! Next stop: Heroic Fucken Jimmy's Nowhere!

All passengers close their eyes and open their mouths and minds and there's a big, bright, all encompassing, cock gobbling flash of Nowhere-Light and the trip takes no more than five seconds of outstretched tongue and what's important here is complete acceptance.

(what will it do to me?)
(don't ask, just swallow it.)
(will it hurt?)
(just swallow it. don't you want to be Nowhere?)
(yes, I do, oh god I do!)
(then open wide, say aaaggghhh...)

And -
Welcome to Nowhere!

Lights and Music and Art and no games and no masks, just your insides hanging out and your outsides tossed away and the wind blows real friendly and there're no alarms or perpetual Sirs, no dog faced rat race mob or the corporate cannon fodder cock blocking mentality.

The Escape Dream Landscape - Welcome to Nowhere!

We (Heroic Fucken Jimmy and I) are out here on the edge of things. The entire rotten globe (todo el fucken mundo!) is a million miles from Nowhere and grinding away in sober stupefaction. Suckers!

Lets just sit around and eat these fabulous squares of paper and to hell with the job and the rent and the car payment! Screw insurance and grocery shopping! Screw the dopey wife and 2.5 screaming children chewing hell out of your ass crying for allowance and dinner and some high maintenance two-story with the manicured lawn!

Heroic Fucken Jimmy says, 'Look, we don't need that typah trash round here. All we need are 500 micrograms of this door opening acid, something cold to drink, some smoke, some fishing line and maybe a hand job every now and again. That's it! After that, we're set!'

And that's the sound of a prophet speaking down from the mountain. And that's a-o-k with me Jimmy boy. I'm beginning to find religion! Shit! Lets toss down some more of that fantastic acid and smoke some more of this green green weed and as for the rest of the world, man, let 'em rust and rot and grind away at the back-breaking wheel of the Stock-Fucken-Life.

Who the hell wants to live like that? asks Heroic Fucken Jimmy.
Not I, said the John, shit.
Who wants to spend their years bowing to the perpetual Sir?
Not I said the John, shit.
And who's going to pull their half-dead ass outa bed today and make the job?
Not! Fucken! I! says the John, like, allofasudden, he's got this new backbone, and its been built entirely outa titanium rods and . . . Braaagght! - Braaagght! - Braaagght! - Braaagght!

And that's the sound of Real (shit, screw and piss) Life going off. The clock reads 6 in the fuck pumping camel hump morning and I'm reeling in the Nowhere dream, the Escape Dream, the toss all you don't need in the trash and pack only the irreplaceable and get off this path of the Stock-Fucken-

Life and I pick up the phone to call the grind, the office, the torture rack iron maiden disembowler deleter and liquefier of soul mind spirit laughter freedom will backbone imagination and let 'em know that I've come down with this rather nasty case of pink eye 'Outrageously contagious. Already infected three people and itches like bloody ass hell and hot tar. Don't wanna risk an outbreak or anything, you know?' and with that out of the way I make another call, 'Hello, Jimmy?' and Jimmy speaks with this spacey, heavily sedated, pondering typah drawl 'Hey man, what's happening - what can I do you for?' 'I was wondering if you had any of those, uh, postage stamps left?' 'Postage stamps, postage stamps . . . Oh, yeah man, lots of stamps, lots and lots of stamps. You wanna mail something?' 'You know it Jim, I need a 3 day express package.' '3 days huh, hmm, yeah, I think I can swing that, yeah, come on down, we'll take a trip together.' 'Sounds good man. Where we off to?' 'Nowhere baby, Nowhere . . .'

ଔ I LIKE THESE NIGHTS

I like these nights -

the free beer
and you put them away
like
breathing
air

up 35 dollars
playing the cards and when you're in the bathroom you
write lines - lines like:

the urine arched clear against the blue backdrop of toilet
water

(or)

happiness -
is a locked door and the loud-LOUD sound
of

complete
silence . . .

bad lines,
but
standing there; zipper down, swaying just a little,
you recite things like this and feel good about yourself,
like you're a real Somebody and
you think of the woman;
all that yellow hair and those lips,
that ass! - hot,
maddening, all you gotta do is call her - but you've been in
the bathroom too long
talking poetry with the walls and a fist beats against the door
you zip up,
get out of there, get back to the table, call for
another drink -

3
long
sips -

light a cigarette
and the
next hand is dealt

5 card stud - 7's wild - 3 dollar ante with 6 people playing -
you look down;

3 Kings & a 7-baby-baby!

"raise 2" and they cast in their lots
while you pull on that cigarette, knock off the beer
and think:

I
really
like these nights

❧ CHINA MOON CURVES

keep People
keep Time

keep heaven and all the
floating lights
of Manhattan

but don't touch
my
China Moon curves

keep the sun
keep the truth

keep your personal black cloud
and dump acid rain on all the howler monkeys, zebra, boa
constrictors and Spanish dancers in
rated X
booths

but stay away from
my
China Moon curves

keep peace
keep sanity

keep tingling nasal passage, high speed heart rate, shaky
hands and
running mouth

just don't fuck with
my
China Moon curves

keep to yourself
keep quiet
keep smoking
keep drinking
keep bleeding all over the carpet and down the stairs - bleed
through the street and let it run thick

for
5 blocks

just make sure you don't get it on
my
China Moon curves . . .

China Moon takes the stage
and the crowd goes wild

China Moon knows all the tricks
back bent
black eyes
staring out from a pale face trapped
behind prison bar legs painted
nails and lips that spell
d-i-s-a-s-t-e-r

I watch China Moon
I watch her curves and whistle with all the other hyenas
I do my imitation of a vacuum cleaner
suck up drinks
then wave my last few dollars - She sees . . .

China Moon watches me
takes panther steps down the lighted runway
does HER imitation of a vacuum cleaner
and sucks up
my last few dollars - Now I see . . .

forget
China Moon-
you can
have her

and her curves.

◌◌ 4 Baby Whites

4 baby whites - fly in the through the window and here sits I
here
sitting I (c'mon already,

MOTHEROF
Shit!)

and

here

I

sit

with open mouth and ready mind, eager body emitting
anticipatory reek - Hello,
my magnificent lows - Hi John - hands wave - fuzzy past and
future blurred and if I'm headed nowhere, then,
fuck,
I'm going with my red eyes buzzing and my buzzing head
blurred tuned into this freak -

freak -

frequency pumped out of

4 baby whites - they smile out from their chalky faces and
twinkle twinkle of their synthetic eyes and here I sit
in stained t-shirt, gambling
on chemicals and on words and hoping that the two
will be enough
to get me out of here alive or at least only half dead or maybe
just comatose and berry red buried under the eerie
orgasmic and fantastical weight

of 4
baby whites - they blanket my rusty gray brains and tell me
it's alright to let the cigarettes burn down to my fingertips:

"It's alright John, let the cigarettes burn down to your
fingertips, it's only a kiss,

a slight kiss,
a far off
and little baby
type pain." and I'm all ears and punk rock tonight
reading Wolfe and Burgess and heavy head syndrome
nodding towards the floor
of some small room
in some big city
and the whole world throws fits
and laughs in hysterics
and sits so damned pretty
in these 4
baby
whites . . .

❧ GIANT STEPS

"Giant steps is what you take
walkin on the moon -

(that's what I was doing,
takin a giant step - NERVOUS - bus ticket bought
and hotel room booked - new bottle and some printed poems -
NERVOUS - back pack stuffed with boxer shorts and rolling
papers - NERVOUS - 3 books and a tape recorder -
NERVOUS - reading out loud in an empty room - voice falls
flat and I curse the ceiling- I'M FUCKEN NERVOUS -
(relax, breathe, it's o.k. baby, just
maintain) - I tell the woman that I'm just not into it tonight,
preoccupied, wandering mind - NERVOUS - I tell The Giant
that I won't make the bar, tense, not feeling a hundred percent
- NERVOUS - and I tell
my self)

I hope my leg don't break
walkin on the moon . . ."

ℂℜ The Reading

I caught the bus in Hempstead. Jumped on at the last minute and took a seat in the back. It was going to be a 6-hour trip, 1 stop to pick up 2 other travelers (a couple; the woman wore a neck brace and smoked a long cigarette, the man came from around the corner in a wheelchair, arms pumping - when he saw the bus about to leave, he leaped from the chair, got behind it and began running - their shirts read 'Las Vegas' and they smelled desperate) Then it was over to the Port Authority in Manhattan. From there I would make the connection to Boston. Once in Boston I had to jump on the Redline subway, walk a couple blocks to the hotel and wait for the Fire. (O.K. I like to dick around when I write, so I'm gonna jump in here and do a little explaining about this Fire thing, but don't worry, I'll bang out this tangent, bring you back to the bus ride, loose ends tied, Fire explained, lickety split, and you won't even notice it. I promise! To start things off here's a quote "what matters most is how well you walk through the Fire.")

Fire: the Fire entity can take shape in a million different things. Fire could be a job interview or a marriage proposal. It could be a side street showdown with someone twice your size or even underwater shark photography. Anything that threatens your person, or shakes your mental foundation, is Fire.

Now, everybody has a special brand of Fire. The first step is identifying which Fire is yours. For me, Fire is a first time poetry reading, in a state with one of the highest populations of writers, some of them professionals no less, and you're a young fuck up - all you've got are some tough lines and a fear of public speaking - that's my Fire.

I was nervous, my entire body tense and sweating, but that was fine, it was expected. I just hadn't realized HOW nervous until I got on the bus in Hempstead.) Every part of me was uptight, even my asshole felt puckered and on edge, by the time I made the Port Authority I was thinking of calling the whole thing off. Saying 'Fuck it!' returning my ticket, canceling my hotel room and going back to my apartment to drink cheap beer and write more bad poems.

After two drinks at the Port Authority bar I was on the bus, still nervous but starting to relax. I opened my bag and took out the material I planned on reading. I went through it once. Not bad, some strong lines and if my delivery was sharp, I'd be all right. (Note: the operative word in that statement was 'if')

The bus began to fill up. I took a seat in the back and next to me was this brunette; curly hair and pale skin, she wore a big sunhat, jeans and a sweater. We pulled out of the terminal, and I started gaining miles on the Fire. That's what I was telling myself; your gaining on the Fire john, your gonna catch it by the tail and make it do what you want. This helped a little.

An hour into the trip I got sick with the chant and started looking around the bus. I took note of the emergency exits and the brunette's legs in the seat next to me. They were thin and I could trace the curves of her knee through the jeans. I watched the legs for ten minutes and then tried to sleep. I closed my eyes and worked on clearing my head with a breathing exercise. I would inhale for 5 seconds, hold it, and exhale for 10. This always worked for me; it would produce a blue, calming effect and leave me with a blank slate type mind. I could feel it coming on, heavy around the frontal lobe, when I heard the noise.

"But, Mommy how long till we get there?"
"Oh soon enough honey, just try and enjoy the ride."
"But I hate the bus, it smells soooo bad. And you're sitting on my winkie-dinkie!"
"Here's winkie, don't worry honey."
"But Mommy, it smells!"

I glance over. Middle-aged single mother and horrible round faced boy. The boy looked
no more than seven and clutched a purple teddy bear, I'm

guessing it's his 'winkie-dinkie', he's got his nose wrinkled while mother pats his head. I close my eyes and do the breathing thing again.
In 2, 3, 4 . . .

"Mommmmmy, now your sitting on my blinkie-blankie and I need it!"
"Oh there, there, here's blinkie-blankie."
"Are we ever gonna get there? It's taking soooo long."
"Yes, soon enough honey. Do you want a snack? Will that make mommy's little boy happy? "

Why is she coddling this kid? Shit! Doesn't she understand that this is why there are so many half-men walking around this world? Jelly-men and Dog-men, Cattle and Sheep-men, men without a drop of steel in their bodies, this is what produces them. Why isn't anybody saying anything? I couldn't handle it; I wanted to scream out 'Tell him to shut up already'. I was getting crazy, thinking: if the entire bus ride is like this - I'm fucked, I'm not going to be relaxed at all. Shit! I was already on edge, this kid is only making it worse and the legs next to me aren't all that special and my asshole all puckered . . . Mother of piss!

I needed to relax. Breathing exercises weren't going to cut it and so I started fantasizing. I shut my eyes and the scene went something like this:

(Bus Scene: - quiet on the set!
Take: 1 – queue the violence
and
Action!)

I would lean over to the brunette with the not so special legs, tell her 'Excuse me baby, let me just squeeze through real quick'. I'd walk up the aisle to where the coddling mother and round child sat. I'd open hand the mother a good one across the mouth, grab that round bastard by the shirt, lift him out of the seat and slam him against the side of the bus, hard enough to knock the air out of him, hard enough to teach him a lesson. Then I'd drop him to the ground and he'd be on all fours, hitching in his chest for air while the mother sat with her mouth open. Grab her by the hair and start moving up the aisle, kicking round boy till he crawled to the back of the bus. Then I'd shove them into the storage closet, telling them things like 'You two got what you deserved!' and 'How do you expect people to relax with all that damn noise? Maybe, next time you'll be a little more considerate of your fellow passengers.'

After that I'd turn back to the bus and all eyes would be on me, after a silent second the applause would start somewhere in the front and work it's way over. They would cheer, saying 'Bravo!' and 'Good work young man! Grade A job!' They'd pat me on the back as I walked to my seat and once I got to my seat the brunette would be there, smiling as I slide across her, she'd say 'You sure are one tough son of a bitch' I'd say something like 'You got that right baby, toughest mother you'll ever meet' then she'd put that sunhat on my lap, work her hand underneath ' So how long you plan on staying in Boston?' I'd answer with a cool smile, shrug my shoulders and fade out the scene.

(Cut!
Perfect, that scene's done, lets send it over to editing.)

I fell asleep with a hard on. In my mind I was seeing blue images and thinking blue thoughts.

Relaxed.

Wake up in Boston - still hard, dick tuck against the belly, belt slide over the shaft-concealed weapon. I make the Redline; jump off at Central Square and the first thing I see is 'King Liquors', walk in the place, fifth of Dewars and a liter of soda, pay 11.30 then back on the street, hailing a cab, Jamaican driver and I tell him 'Gateway Inn, east on Route 2', twenty dollars and I check in the place -

"Room 207 Mr. Dempsey, do you have any bags?"

In the room I lay out my material, take out all the pretty poesy that I'm going to read and check my tape recorder 'testing, testing, hello - mic check'. With everything in order, I mix a drink. Knock it off and decide on a quick shower -

bus scum and nervous sweat.

I undress, mix a second drink, grab my papers, the two bottles and head for the bathroom. Naked, I sit on the toilet. Reading out loud I work through the set twice. I start with 'Travel Log' and end on 'Empty', my voice echoes off the bathroom tiles and fills the place. I finish drink number two and hop in the shower.

I turn the faucets to lukewarm and lay down in the tub, the water shoots from the showerhead and splashes my face and shoulders, runs across my chest and down to my crotch, covering my legs, and the two bottles float in the water. I pick them up, unscrew both and take a shot of the Dewars to relax and one of soda to chase. I was feeling good, I would be ready for the Fire, I opened my mouth and yelled it 'Ready Mother! Anytime you want!' I took another shot, swished it around my mouth and spit it across my chest, took the bottle and poured a little over my head. I was feeling like a champ. I was going to knock these babies dead on their asses tonight, nothing could stop me, I pinched my nipples and started giggling, squeezed my balls with my right hand and had a drink with the left. I was ready, damned ready!

Jumped outa the tub, toweled off and called the guy in charge of the reading:

"Hello."
"Greg, what's happenin man? It's john."
"John, how's it goin? You make it in alright?"
"Yeah, yeah, no problems. The ride was a bit of a bitch but I was able to manage."
"Good, good. I'm down at Borders right now. I'm having a drink and waiting on this other guy to show. You want to come down and meet us?"
"Yeah, definitely. I been sitting in this room for the last three hours, jacking off and drinking shit, I'm ready to get out of here."

He laughed, gave me directions and twenty minutes later, I banged my way into the place. At the door 'Sorry sir, no smoking allowed', I inhaled, deep, and ground my butt out on

the curb. Crowded. Shit! I don't even know what these guys
look like, how am I gonna get a drink in this place, and why
in the fuck can't I smoke in here? I scan the bar, see a head
nod and walk over.

"John?"
"Hey, what's goin on?"
"Not much, still waitin on this guy, you want a drink?"

(Hey, reader, what the hell do you think?)

"Yeah, 2 Dewars and coke."
"Not in Boston man, you can only get 1 at a time here."

(Mother!)

The bartender brings it over and I do the fish trick, 1 sip and
the glass is empty.

"Bring me another."

We put em down for an hour or so and then it's time to make
the reading. I get in Greg's car and he drives over. It's a small
joint, blue walled on the outside and placed in a residential
area. Paintings covered every inch of the inside, Monet look-
a-likes and skyline scenes. There was also a couple of
photographs but I don't remember what they were of. Greg
and another person, I don't remember his name either, went
to work setting up chairs and adjusting lights. It was almost
time for the Fire.

Beer was sold out of a cooler and they didn't give you any
shit about ordering two at a time. I put them away and waited
for my slot.

I had signed up for the last fifteen minutes of open mic, there
were four readers ahead of me and listening to their material I
told myself 'Baby, these guys are only 1/3 writer, they
wouldn't take a shot in the nuts if it meant five pages of
serious material, they wouldn't know what to do with it, but
you johnny boy, you're a different story, you're gonna be
death from above, you're a fucken tiger baby, a powerhouse,
you're unstoppable, this is your god damned destiny!' And as
the last reader finished, I got up, and marched into the Fire.

(Okay people lets not screw this up, we're gonna do the Fire
scene. This one is gonna cost us, big time, it's gonna suck up
resources that are already low and it better be perfect. I want
one take; you got that, just one.

Fire Scene: - quiet on the god damned set!
Take: 1 - queue the Fire
and
Action!)

I stumbled up to the Fire. It was a wooden chair under a
spotlight. The other readers had been standing, facing the
audience and acting real professional. I dropped into the
chair, set up my tape recorder, looked out over the crowd, and
started:

Travel Log

I was a Vietnam vet, in Cairo,
Egypt, where -
I learned to drive like a maniac,
drink liquid codeine,
and break
a belly dancer's wrist . . .

The applause came in, heavier than I had expected and
instead of loosening me up it set me on edge. I started
sweating. I had gotten through the first one alright but I didn't
feel right about pushing it any further, I wanted to get up
from the chair and bolt for the door, there was a long pause
and I looked towards the window.

Something like magic happened. It seemed that as soon as my
eyes turned to the glass, the sky opened up and began
dropping snow.

I took it as a sign and kept pushing.

I read 'Some times' without any energy; I had lost my pep,
my zip and jazz. I kept making mistakes and every time I
tripped up my words I would stop reading and yell 'Mother'
or 'Fuck'. The sweat was pouring from every part of me and
all those drinks were playing with my vision. I hauled ass
through the rest of it, more applause, undeserved, sympathetic

and I jumped onto the next, now I only had one thing in mind: Escape the Fire!

I did 'Letch', 'Wake up call, 5am in Florida', 'Where are we going with this?' and every one of them stank. These were good pieces. Well written and from the gut, only one problem, my reading was shit. I kept losing my place, missing entire stanzas, cursing when there wasn't a need for it and cheapening what I had busted my ass to produce. There was blood in those words, MY blood god damnit, and I was letting it all out, letting it pour across the floor and down the drain, letting it disappear without making a single splash.

MOTHERFUCKME!

I finished the set, shitty and beaten, my confidence shot and my outlook shit. I was telling myself that it was over, wasn't meant to be, I'm a has been that never was, a joke, I'm no better than the . . . APPLAUSE, mad clapping that seemed genuine and I looked out over the faces, and whispered, real soft, thank you.

Throughout the reading I had been sort of dropping my papers on the ground. The other guys/gals had been professional about it, bringing folders and binders of stapled material, but me, I couldn't be that prepared. I just read down one side and let go of the page, it would sail around on the air currents before settling on the floor. Now that the reading was finished I saw the mess, there were papers all over the place, scattered at my feet and under chairs. I leaned over to collect them and almost went down on my face; my equilibrium was a laughing matter, my legs unsteady and I was making these grunting noises. It was if I was performing some amazing physical act that required superhuman strength. Bullshit. I was drunk, too drunk and as I fought my way back to my seat, I felt waves of nausea, working through my body.

I sat down, lit a cigarette and tried to regain control.

(Cut! Cut!
Good job guys. Couldn't have gone any better. Lets send this bit over to screening, and wrap it up, another page or so and

it's Miller time!)

40 minutes later the reading was over, the main features did
their bit real smooth, the lights came on and I was back in
control of myself. A couple of young guys walked over to me
-

"Hey man, good shit, some of it really blew me away."
"Thanks, thanks, much appreciated."
"You published or anything?"
"Me, ha, no I'm not published, another 5 years or so."
"Oh, o.k. Well, take it easy man! Hope to see you read
again!"

I can't say I liked the exchange, compliments are great and all
but I was never good at receiving them. Then this other one
comes over, a writer for some magazine, short, cute with the
dark hair and holding a money chin -

"Definitely different, good, but different."
"Oh, why thank you baby."
"No problem. Hey, I'm goin out with Greg and some other
people after they clean up here, you should come along."
"Yeah, I think I might."

Greg and some other people cleaned up the place, I walked
around and made more small talk, finally it was time to take
off. We made 'The Middle East', ordering domestic beer and
French fries. I was in control of myself, I knew I wasn't
going to puke but I was in no way sober. I felt shitty about the
reading. I knew I could've done better, fucken knew it! And I
wanted to tell these people that, I wanted to shut off all the
noise in the place, set up a chair in the center of the room and
jump back into the Fire.

It obviously never happened. Instead I talked shit and lied
about my age, told some crazy
stories (true ones) and threw out some stock phrases that I
had. Here's an example:

Look baby, I'm headed towards one of three places - young
death in a small room, middle age on an empty street, or old
age in a three story, living the good life off all the money

people pay me for my goddamned words.

Nothing special, typical dempsey shit. 2 am came down and it was time to leave. I walked with Greg and the magazine chick for a few blocks till they got to their cars. I tried a couple of bad lines in an attempt to get her to come back to the hotel with me. No dice. My head was screwed from booze and I came off like some college fuck with soft hands and a hard on. We shook goodbye, I got in the car with Greg and he drove me over to the hotel.

"Well, it was good meeting you Greg, thanks for the opportunity."
"No problem man. Come up again sometime."
(There was probably more dialogue then this, but like I said before, I really don't remember.)

I got out of his car and stumbled into the hotel lobby. The night manager was smiling and I made straight for him -

"Hey buddy, how's it hangin? Look I need a wake up call, 6:40, 7 o'clock - got a bus to catch."
"What time did you want the call?"
"Give me one at 6:40 and another at 7. Just to make sure you know?"
"O.k. What room are you in?"
"207! The dempsey suite!"
"O.k. sir, room 207, 1 call at 6:40 and once again at 7, will that be all?"
"No, what time is breakfast in this place?"
"We begin serving at 6:30 sir."
"Alright, I'll see you there."

I barely made it up the stairs, crawling up the last flight on all fours and then through the hallway. There was a moment of serious panic when I couldn't find the door key; I began tearing at my pockets and taking off my shoes when I realized where I had hid it. (When you live like this you learn that you will inevitably lose something when you go out. It could be something small like a lighter or a button, or it could be something big, something like your wallet, or your mind, or your hotel key for instance and once this happens enough times, you start to wise up. You learn to hide the things that will fuck you if they were to get lost. This is what I did here.) I crawled back through the hall, all the way to where the door for the stairs stood, I lifted the edge of the carpet and pulled out my key.

I'm not sure of everything else that happened after that. I know that I smashed my tape recorder at some point. I'm also pretty sure that I walked up and down the hall, banging on doors and propositioning anyone that would answer. If a woman opened the door, regardless of what she looked like, I'd say 'Hey baby, you interested in riding the wildest prick this side of the Mason-Dixon?' And if it was a man 'Hey mother, you interested in taking on the most dangerous fists Europe has ever seen?' No takers, from either sex.

I tried every door I came across and snapped awake the next day-on the floor, phone ringing.

"Hello, Mr. Dempsey, this is your wake up call."
"Thanks, I'm up."
"Would you still like a 7 o'clock call back?"
"Nah, it'll be o.k."

I packed up, threw the tape recorder guts into the trash (somehow the tape wasn't damaged - what did you think, I got this all down from memory?) grabbed a croissant from the breakfast table and ran for the subway. By the time I made the bus terminal, found the gate and sat down I was a dead man; dehydrated and half blind from the heavy booze and little sleep. I fell into the chair, closed my eyes and passed out.

5 hrs later I was home, back in Manhattan with the street freaks and cross dressers. I had made it through the Fire. I can't say I walked out the other end free and clear, but I hadn't been arrested, hadn't been thrown off the bus and there wasn't a black eye winking back at me from the mirror, the reading had gone like shit and I'd probably never be asked back, but Oh Mother, did I feel like a writer.

◌ INSTINCT

If its 4 in the morning
If its broken

I know -

If its puking
If its falling up stairs with bloody lips and laughing

I know -

If its yelling at the television
If its stolen

If its too pink

If its too green

If its fishing for lines or jumping from windows

If its cross dressed and there's no denying the adams apple,
wide shoulders,
big hands or chin whiskers

I know -

That I just typed
a bad poem - john

◌ CHICAGO

Chicago woke up that morning feeling horrible. He
immediately took note that he was naked; an abused condom
hung loose from his dick and his head was pounding. The
headache let him know he had been drinking heavy. The
condom let him know that he had spent the night with Cassie.
He could never trust Cassie. She had screwed more men than
taxes and roulette combined. Whenever she called him to
come over he didn't know if he was laying it to her for the
first time that night, or if he was just the cleanup crew.

Chicago could hear her moving around in the other room. The clicking of heels said that she was dressed - and Cassie knew how to dress; she'd wear tight little things that could drive a man crazy at twenty yards. Tiny skirts that moved just right when she walked. Or the half buttoned shirt that showed just the right amount of cleavage, and would leave half a New York block with a hard on. She loved doing this. She was the type that could kill a man with a closed lip kiss, leave him standing with his eyes shut while she walked out the door with someone else.

Chicago got out of the bed, peeled the condom off and put on his shorts. From the other room Cassie yelled:

"Hey, you finally woke up."
"Yeah - you got any aspirin?"
"Sure, check the bathroom."

Chicago found the aspirin, chewed three tablets and chased them with cold water from the tap. As he swallowed he heard the doorbell. Then he heard Cassie telling someone that she'd be right out.

"Where you going?"
"Oh, I thought I told you. John is taking me out today. We're going shopping and then over to that new bar on Waverly - I heard they have a whole wall that's a fish tank. I've been dying to see it!"
"But I though that we we're…"
"I gotta run - don't forget to lock up."

This was typical Cassie, out the door and down the hall before he was dressed. Chicago sat there in his shorts and asked himself: Why? Why did he love her like this? Why did she have such a strong hold on him? He knew he would kill for Cassie, Shit! He had come close to doing so before. It was right after he had first met her. She had taken him home on a Thursday night and by sun up Friday, he was infatuated. On Saturday he made the downtown bar and saw her kissing a suit.

Chicago didn't care much for suits, and this one, sitting there with his face plastered to hers, made him see red. He walked up and without saying a word, started throwing punches. He caught him on the chin with a hard right and the suit dive-bombed to the ground. Chicago followed him down with the left and started in with the kicking.

It took Larry the bartender, Cassie and one of the regulars to pull him off. When Larry told him to go out the back door, he grabbed Cassie by the arm and moved.

Once they got outside she shook loose and laid an open hand across his face.

"Who do you think you are? You can't just walk in a bar and beat the shit out of someone like that! What the fuck is wrong with you?"

And Chicago didn't have an answer. Well, he knew what was wrong with him, but what was he going to say: hey I've only known you three days but I think I'm in love with you? That doesn't work in this city. Women around here steered clear of the emotional types.

He did the only thing he could; he lit a cigarette and shoved his hands into his pockets.

"Are you going to answer me?"
"Look, I'm sorry. I don't know why I did that - it just happened."
"What, did you think that after the other night you owned me or something?"
"No, not at all. It was a mistake. I apologize."
"I can't believe you did that. And I was having such a good time too - you just walked up and ruined it."
"Look Cassie - I really didn't mean to. Like I said before - I'm sorry."

It went back and forth like this. It was a bad scene and ended with Cassie saying she never wanted to see him again. She walked off in one direction and Chicago left in the other.

A month later Chicago sat in the downtown bar. Larry was serving the drinks and Chicago, depressed and looking broken, made them disappear. It was closing in on seven o'clock when Cassie walked in the place. She scanned the bar, spotted him, took the stool on his left, and asked for cranberry vodka.

They didn't make any conversation, just sat there; putting down the drinks, and when Larry yelled, "Last call!" she got up. Chicago followed.

That was eight months ago.

Now, Chicago was no saint himself. When he started this thing with Cassie he had been sleeping with Maria for almost a year. Maria was from the Philippines and loved him like mad. She radiated love for him. Here's the way it worked in this triangle - Chicago was to Maria, what Cassie was to Chicago (image of a dog chasing it's tail).

Maria thought Chicago was one of the only REAL men she had ever been with. He always knew the right things to say to her. And no matter how many times he kissed her forehead before falling asleep at night, she always felt like crying when he did it. That kiss made her feel so small, like she was 4 years old, and that, while he wasn't exactly a father figure, he would protect her, like he was a guardian of some sort, meant just for her.

Chicago mused over this while getting dressed and decided that he'd stop and see Maria before going home.

He got on the street; the hangover was bad; sunlight hurting his eyes and the headache seemed worse. He took the subway, four stops, and jumped off at Canal St.

Maria lived in a small, clean apartment. She would buy flowers once a week and fill vases and water bowls with everything from snapdragons to tiger lilies and baby irises. This made the apartment seem bigger and gave it the feel of NOT being in the city. This was important to Chicago. It was a change of pace from his apartment. His place had only one working light at any given time. It was dark and the faucets dripped. Bottles and cans sat in large mounds in the corners and by the couch. The smell of stale smoke was constantly hanging in the air and the carpet was no more than a multi colored stain; puke greens, wine reds, discharge yellows - depressing. Chicago liked the fresh, clean feel of Maria's place and he was thinking about flowers and crisp sheets when he rang her bell.

Maria buzzed him in, and he stood in front of her door less than two minutes later.

"Hey Chicago. Wow! You look like shit!"
"Thanks - rough night."
"I can see that. Come inside, I was just getting ready for work."

Chicago walked in the place and inhaled roses. As soon as he got inside his mind was in the country; the subway was light years away, cab drivers and their cursing mouths, young hoods and switchblades, all of it, gone, disappeared. Here were horse carriages and banjos. Here was slow life and clean air.

"Why don't you call in, take the day off?"
"Can't Chicago, I need the money. But you know you can stay if you want."

He already had his shoes off. He worked at the shirt and belt and soon he was stretched under clean sheets.

Maria's a real good girl he thought to himself, I should stop chasing Cassie and make a go at it with her - she doesn't have a trace of the killer in her eyes, she'd never think of hurting me - and here I am, rolling out of one bed and into another. Ah fuck, I'm just like all these guys on the street, just another shit, hell-bent on pipedreams and pussy.

This was a bad thought pattern to be following. It was the hangover talking, he told himself. You need to sleep this off.

"Hey Chicago, if you're here when I get back I can make you some dinner. Maybe we can rent a movie or something."

And even with his conscience hounding him, his mind turned back to Cassie - she wouldn't be home from her date with John till much later, plus Maria was one hell of a cook.

"That sounds like a good idea. I'll stick around till you get home."

Maria came into the bedroom and kissed him. She looked into his eyes and drank him in; ohhhh, she loved him so much, too much. Why? Why did she love him like this? Why did he have such a strong hold on her? (image of a dog chasing it's tail). She kissed him once more, sighed, a drop forming in the corner of one eye, and left for work. Maria didn't want to lose Chicago, and she knew that if she confronted him, it would happen.

Maria knew all about Cassie, she could smell the guilt, coming off Chicago in waves.

Chicago slept three hours and woke up feeling better. The aspirin had worked on his head and his conscience had quieted down. He went to Maria's fridge and grabbed two bottles of beer. Chicago opened one and took a long pull; he started to feel even better. He lit a cigarette, took another pull, another - better. Soon both bottles were empty and Chicago started thinking about Cassie again. He didn't know what she saw in that John character. He was some writer, or some thing, that wrote these horrible poems. Cassie had let him read a few and he just didn't get it. They all seemed one sided, full of jaded observations and sexist. Shit, they didn't even rhyme!

"Aren't poems supposed to rhyme?" he had asked her.
"Oh Chicago, you just don't know anything about art." She told him

Fuck art! What did he care about sculptures or paintings or, or . . . or bad poems for that matter. All he cared about was Cassie. Wasn't that the only thing that mattered?

He knew she wouldn't be home but he called anyway. The phone rang twice and an out of breath Cassie answered. Chicago thought he had caught her in the middle of a sweaty interlude and immediately went to hang up. The receiver was kissing the cradle when he heard her say his name.

"Chicago? Chicago is that you?"

He picked the phone back up.

· 76 ·

"Hey honey, how come you're home already?"

"Oh my god! I just ran 5 blocks to get here."

"What happened? Are you o.k.? Did that fucken guy do something to you?"

"No, no. Look I'm fine; just got a little scared is all. Ugh - John is such a dick! You can't go anywhere with him!"

"Why, what happened baby?"

"Well we went shopping and I could tell he was on something. His eyes were all spaced out and he kept knocking things off the rack. So I said we should go get something to drink, you know? I was figuring it would calm him down."

"Then what happened?"

"Well we got down to that new place on Waverly I was telling you about, and ooh Chicago you should've seen that fish tank wall, it was wild! They had SO many fish and they were SO pretty, they were all different colors and this one had a crazy, long snout that . . . "

"Look Cassie, just tell me what happened with John, I don't wanna hear about the fish."

"Oh, yeah, well, we got down to the bar and started drinking. Things were fine for an hour or so then that fuck goes over to the jukebox and puts on some music, some idiot country shit, then he gets up on the bar and starts yelling 'I'm the Mermaid King! I'm the New Year's Princess! No one can stop me!' He's loud too, knocking over glasses and telling people they're worthless. Then the bartender grabs his ankle and he kicks him right in the face! Can you believe that? Right in his face! There was blood all over the bar and he just kept at it 'I'm Billy fucken Gates on coke! I'm the Prince of Egypt! You people are the walking dead!' He acts like he's some kind of somebody, you know, like a rock star or something. So I just picked up my shit and got out of there."

"What a dick!"

"And that's not all of it! I got down two blocks and this bottle comes flying through the air, almost hits me in the head, and there's John running up the block, screaming at me 'You whore!' and something about loyalty. I was running I was so scared. He followed me to my apartment and now he's outside yelling."

As if on cue, Chicago heard it over the phone 'You dirty whore!'

"I'm gonna kill that guy!"
"Oh no you won't, you're gonna stay out of this."
"What the fuck do you mean stay out of it? No one talks to my girl like that! I'm on my way over!"
"Look, first off I'm nobody's . . . "

Chicago hung up the phone. He knew what she was going to say and he didn't want to hear it. Maria and her flowers and dinner and the clean sheets were nowhere in his thoughts. He moved fast, got dressed and was out the door in less than a minute, a quick train ride and he was racing up the block to Cassie's apartment. Out on the street there was no sign of John - good. He rang the buzzer and Cassie let him in. When he got to her door she was standing in the frame.

"I don't know why you came here, he left about 5 seconds after I hung up with you."
"Because baby. He can't talk to you like that."
"Why don't you let me decide who can and can't talk to me in what way. Besides I handled it myself."
"Oh did you?"
"Yeah, I told him that I was calling the cops and he just took off. Huh, it figures, all that macho shit, I just mentioned the word police and he took off."
"Well it could've been worse you know."
"Yeah, but it wasn't. Now are you gonna take me out for a drink or are we gonna stand in the hall all day?"

What Chicago really wanted to do was kiss her. Kiss her like mad and lay down in bed with her. He wanted to hold her and love her the way it was supposed to be done, tell her that she didn't need guys like John, or any other guys for that matter, just him.

No chance. When Cassie was drinking she only wanted one

thing: more to drink.

"Let's go baby, we'll make the downtown bar and see Larry."

Chicago and Cassie left the bar at 3 o'clock that morning. He had spent his cash and then run up the tab for another 50 bucks. Cassie was sloppy drunk and he half carried - half walked her home. They got to the apartment building and Cassie fished through her purse for the keys. After 5 minutes she found them, worked it into the lock, walked in, and shut the door behind her. She didn't even glance back at him as she walked towards her apartment. Chicago stood there, watching her through the glass, he sighed, a drop forming in the corner of one eye. When he saw that she got in the apartment, he turned and started home.

Chicago didn't want to lose Cassie, and he knew that if he confronted her, it would happen - (once again, here's that image of a dog).

He got back to his apartment and saw the 'new message' light blinking. There were 2 messages. He hit play:

"O.k. Chicago, I didn't want to do this over the phone, but if you were in front of me right now, I know I wouldn't go through with it. Look, I LOVE you damnit, I mean I REALLY LOVE you. I'd give up the world to have you for myself, but that'll never happen. I know you love that other girl. I know you were with her tonight even though you said you'd stay here and wait for me. Do you understand, that every time I walk away from you, I cry? I've been crying for over a year now Chicago. I just CAN'T DO IT ANYMORE. At first I thought you would come around, that maybe you'd see how much I cared for you and break it off with her. I'm so stupid. After tonight I don't think you're ever going to feel for me the way I feel for you. So here it is. I don't want you to call me anymore. Don't try to see me or stop by my apartment. You've killed me enough for one life. Thanks allot Chicago."

Fuck! She sounded hurt; her voice was all tears in the back of the throat and he knew she meant it. Maria was lost to him.

There would be no more lotus flowers floating in glass bowls of water, no more of that clean feel or crisp sheets.

No more Maria.

The second message began to play:

"Hey Chicago, it's Cassie. Look, I don't really know how to say this the right way so I'll just spit it out. I'm in love with John. I don't think I should see you anymore. I know how you feel about me and I almost felt that way for you at one time, but ever since I met John, I see myself caring more and more for him and less for you. It's not right. My whole life I've been yelling about my freedom and now I know why; I hadn't met the right person yet. But with John I just know. Every part of me knows. We're meant for each other and that's all there is to it. Can you understand that? And I know he's bad, I know he's violent and self-centered and crazy and a million other things but it just doesn't matter to me. I'm sorry Chicago, if I hurt you I didn't mean to, I swear I didn't. Please take care of yourself."

And Chicago sat there, half drunk, with his face wet and no love, thinking of Maria and Cassie and John and when the phone rang he answered without any energy.

"Hello."
"Chicago?" (a female voice)
"Yeah, who's this?"
"It's Lisa, we met at Brian's party a couple of weeks back."
"Oh, hey Lisa. How'd you get my number?"
"You gave it to me that night, remember?" (yeah he remembered, Lisa was one serious number, a long yellow with the good body, actually, she looked just like Cassie)
"Yeah - yeah, now I do. So what's happening?"
"Not much, I didn't wake you up did I?"
"No, not at all."
"I was just sitting here and I came across your number, figured I'd call and see if you wanted to go out one night."
"Yeah sure, anytime you want."
"How about Tuesday? You know that new place down on Waverly, I heard they have an entire wall that's a fish tank!"

(just like Cassie)
"Tuesday's cool with me. How about 8?"
"That's perfect, I'll see you there."

Chicago hung up the phone, now he was thinking of Cassie
and Lisa and he started singing.

"I've got Two women
You can't tell 'em apart
I got one in my bosom
And the other one is in my heart

Well that one
in my bosom
She lives in Tennessee
But that one in my heart
Well,
She don't give a darn for me"

* (Lyrics from a White Stripes song)

ෲ I WAS CONCERNED ABOUT MY HEALTH
AND SO I . . .

Made an appointment for a physical,
then called the dentist, ophthalmologist, and a good ear man
in Denver.
Proctologist tells me to show up at 2 with a referral and my
insurance card.
Pathologist at 3, psychologist on Wednesday, podiatrist is
booked till next week - Balls-no,

actually

feet. Psychoanalyst on the upper west side charges 75 an hour
and wears expensive striped
ties - something about my mother and my friend claims to be
a socialist. Neurosurgeon next Friday and I'm a self-licensed
anesthesiologist. Dermatologist says he can squeeze me in,

but the chiropractor is away, the French Riviera
and that makes me wonder
about where he puts his hands.
The cardiologist is home
with a sprained back and my woman
wants to be a geologist. I'm a cunnilinguist with 2
appointments as an internalist and there's a pulmonary man in
Brooklyn that's supposed to be one of the best, wants to
check the reactivity
of the bronchial and vascular tissues as well as my
enzymatic pathways. I pull a three-day drunk and wake up at
the free clinic, name's Swazzy, Bret Swazzy, I tell the
volunteer nurse, I'm in the catering business and lately, I, uh
have found myself
in uh,
some compromising positions with um, some
unwholesome type girls. I clinch my teeth
while she draws blood,
lubricates a cotton swab,
and inserts it

halfway up the shaft

of my half-hard

dick, gives me a blue card and tells me to call the number on
the back,
takes about ten business days,
it's an automated system, just enter your test ID and a
prerecording will give you the results, thank you and have a
nice day, my fingers crossed and please o please god mantra
leaking out of my mouth.

Get home, turn on the television, and there's a meteorologist.

I pick up the phone
and call an estranged woman, she's a sadomasochist. I crack
the first fifth
of the fourth Friday and think about how in college
I used to drink with this tall German. Now that guy,

he was a Marxist.

❧ ANOTHER DRUNKEN WRITE

The whole world feels better when I'm this fucked up:

- Frusciante
knew what he was doing. Listen to nothing but water for ten
days straight. No telephone, no television, no radio, no
nothing - just water,

it's a cleansing process.

- I'm lost
in a million summer time hues. Between the trees and the sun,
shift from brown
to green
to yellow
to red - just colors,

it's enough to make you believe in the gods.

- This life
can't be more than a stepping stone.
Slit wrist - swan dive - pill mouth overdose will bring u up a
notch - just a notch,

it's a feeling of detachment.

- I've become quite the slob,
piss in the sink without washing the hands - have I been
wearing this shirt since Monday(?)

Ah -
Screw it(!)
Screw what(?) random chicks with a nightclub libido and
who knows,
where I'll be five years from now - just placing a bet,

I've always
liked to gamble.

- Who am I?
Just a nobody. I've got a computer that lets me type like this.
I've got a mind

that let's me think these thoughts and my sister's a lawyer,
says she'll help me out
with any legal troubles
that I might run into - just a connection,

I need
all the friends
that I can get.

- Baby,
I have a problem with not going over board - crushed
celebrex swims in the beer - and this allows me to drive 15
miles
to meet a guy about some coke - just a habit,

every now and then,
I wonder where I'm headed.

- Ending: It's 1 in the morning. I'm drunk enough to see the
future

and I would like to make a few predictions:

1) Mr. Dempsey will be out of the office tomorrow.
2) Mr. Dempsey will wake up with spinning head and vomit
mouth.
3) Mr. Dempsey will finish this poem, read over it,
and fucking hate it - just the way it works,

it all
amounts to absolutely nothing.

CЯ Monday Morning

I was in the shower
adjusting knobs
and lathering balls
(the balls are always first)
and turning the water handle
I heard a mad squealing of pipes,
the shower head shook, real violent,

and then
began pouring snakes
(small snakes;
baby rattlers and diamond
backs, tiny copper heads, pythons
and corn snakes) and I left for work
without washing up, walked five blocks for the train,
and got on the platform, where
this Jamaican waited;
pretending to read (a copy of 'Death in the Afternoon' and I
knew he was only pretending because his eyes never moved
(I pretended to read 'Shogun' and you could tell I was
pretending because my eyes never moved)) and when the
downtown A
pulled into the station
the Jamaican tried flanking me along the right,
I saw his hands,
reaching out for the big push,
and I spun on fast heels, right arm
up for the block and he must've seen me reacting because at
the last second
he backed away
and I got on the train,
nice
and
easy.

I took that train 4 stops, hopped off at West 3rd, and made the
coffee stand, (the regular coffee guy wasn't there, in his place
was this new character; shifty brown eyes and tight mouth)
and waiting in line I saw that he had one cup set aside,
and when my turn came up,
I called for a large regular and he pulled that set aside cup,
mixed my coffee,
then handed it over.

I took the cup,
got around the corner,
lifted the lid,
and inhaled;

almonds,

light smell of almonds
and I tossed that cup at the next trashcan,
walked 2 more blocks,
turned
right,
then left,
and made the office.

It was between the fourth and fifth floor that the elevator
came to a halt,
steel cables grinding,
and the lights went out, I heard a stealthy zipping sound, (and
that sound told me all I needed to know; there was one body,
medium build, sliding down the right cable. I noted the trap
door on the ceiling, the direction in which the hinges would
allow it to open, and positioned myself in a defensive crouch,
knees bent, with arms at the ready.)
a soft landing,
trap door swings open,
reveals outline of a shaved head
(and here I'll throw you a picture: of a tiger,
stalking prey,
feline body
low to the ground - hind quarters twitch,
killer eyes focus,
lock on target
and . . .) pounce as I come up from the crouch,
hands grip the shaved head,
downward pull,
momentum works in my favor
and as the body comes down, I follow with the shoulders,
hands position the neck,
knees bend,
a whiff of aftershave as the body sails past,
and then the dull thud
of unconsciousness.

Not wasting any time, I climbed up through the trap door,
took hold of the cable,

and using the walls of the elevator chute as footholds,
made it to the sixth floor - there I pulled out a pocketknife,
slid it between the elevator doors,
and with a turning motion,
forced them apart.

The gap was wide enough for my fingers,
then I had my foot through, my leg,
my waist and chest,
right arm, head,
left arm, and for the finale, (drum roll here)
my left leg.

I walked:

down the hall,
through big double doors -

inserted key, turned handle,
switched on lights and . . . Bang! 2 badgers come running at
me,
full speed,
claws out and rabid foam dripping.

I react fast,
and with a slam of the door,
catch the lead badger around the torso, come down with a
heel to the spine,
crunch of bones, small jet of blood from badger mouth, a
final claw at the air,
and then

complete

stillness.

I hold the door closed, look around,
see a box of copy paper and prop it against the door,
walk back out
through
big double doors,
down
the hallway,
and decide on the stairs.

I hit the street, with thoughts of the downtown bar.

My feet did the rest and soon I was at the place -

the eye-opener crowd
was putting down the high-octane coffee
and I pull up to the bar,
call for beer, light cigarette
and

Duck! when shiny steel flashes across my peripheral,
side step with a crash of heel against the upper part of the
assailant's foot,
spring up with a strong right, followed by a chop to the wrist,
shiny steel drops
and I
leave without getting my beer.

Back on the street,
heading for subway, looking over shoulder,
I was
watching out for Jamaicans,
badgers,
bald-headed assassins and undercover coffee agents.

I saw none,

got on the uptown A,
4 stops,
got off the uptown A,
5 blocks,
deli on the corner produces 6 tall boys without incident.

I make the apartment - call the office and give em the
'I'm sick - puking - with virus and fever' routine - open the
first tall boy,
take a long pull,
and wait for Tuesday.

ℭℛ REGRESSION

We snorted 3 grams of coke
and screwed like jackals -

bare teeth, heavy sweat and the loud snarling, it was all
very
animalistic -

and afterwards,
the light
swarms in from the window
and we stare at each other, panting . . .

I was home,
back in the jungle where I belonged.

ℭℛ SELF-DESTRUCT-KID

Self-Destruct-Kid steps in thru batwing doors - blink of
an eye captures picture like some Self-Destruct-Camera
trick - CLICK CLICK:

breath hangs stale as bar smoke, situation hopeless,
face of the inevitable, gallows march, small smile and
pinky ring gleam, last train departed, missed while
standing next to a dead man; tells the best tales - high
heels and switchblade mouth, zipper teeth crunch on
empty pants -

Self-Destruct-Kid blends with photo, thumbs in belt,
gap in teeth spills Self-Destruct-Words -

letters squeeze into mold, form death-wish sentence
easy as Christmas suicide, swan dive conversation
magnifies 15 stories of the Escape Dream: Escape
Dream is easy way out, is one way road, is dead end
street -

Self-Destruct-Kid turns on carousal heels; low-slung
holster empties itself into Self-Destruct-Hands -

.45 caliber drops population simple as empty bottle,
jack knife with bone handle as rear guard, does this
trick real casual, flicks wrist and blade dances quick
silver through empty space, delivers 10 slashes and
spins round like boomerang, returns to open palm like
some dog being called home, 10 men bloom rose
neckties -

Self-Destruct-Kid at a loss for ammunition, jack knife
lost in a western chest, calls up last ditch effort of
stomach acid -

blasts across the photo with reptile hiss, flash dance of
dissolve tapped out in sickly green Morse (-.. . .- - .... /
-... -.-- / .- -.-. .. -..) bowling pin analogy tells of bodies
dropped under the August sun, 2 days from now is vulture
time, wild dog time, snap snarl of the big feast, canine
teeth and rabid beak, pull of string/flesh -

"Not a hungry face in house Sir"

Self-Destruct-Kid is last man standing, scents out the
jackknife with nostril quiver,
pulls unused shells from corpse gun belts, steps back
thru batwing doors, and all we're left with
is a footstep imprint, marching into
the Self-Destruct-Desert

ℂℛ PHOTO SHOOT

The idea was to get some pictures together - had a collection
coming out - poems

(is that what these are?)

and talking to the editor
it was decided that a few pictures

would really
give the thing some life (you see,

death,

runs real heavy
through all these lines and
a certain type of

balance

is needed) So I got my hands on a camera,
picked up the phone,
punched 7 buttons and got the woman:

"Look baby, I need you to come over, today's picture day,
just like when we were in school. I wanna snap a few shots of
you."
"Of me?"
"Yeah of you. Now chop-chop, were losing light!" (all of a
sudden,
I'm a photographer)
"John . . . "
"Yeah?"
"Before I come over . . . "
"What?"
"What exactly, are these pictures for?"
"I'm starting an amateur porn site. You're gonna be my star
model baby. What do you think of that?"
"I think I'm going to hang up the phone."
"No, no, don't do that. I'm just kidding. Look, I got a new
camera and I want to try it out, that's all."
"Oh . . . well then, what should I wear?"
"The usual, I want this to have a real natural look."
"Oooh, can I wear my new shirt?"
"Baby, you can tape tinfoil to your titties if you want, just
hurry up!'
"What did you just say to me?"
"Three hundred people livin down in West Virginia."
"What?"
"Have no idea of all these thoughts that lie within ya."
"What the hell are you saying?"

"Nothin, I'm just singing honey."
"Oh, I like it when you sing. O.k. I'll be right over!"

Whenever a woman tells me 'I'll be right over', I know I've
got 45 minutes to an hour before she makes her entrance.

I made the store,
picked up soda (for that half bottle
of white rum
sitting by my bed), 6 talls, a box of mediums and 2 cans of
tuna - the checkout girl
had this marvelous little ass, and nice eyes, and when I got
home, I mixed a strong drink, had a few strokes
and 20 minutes later
the woman showed up. We burned some
expensive
green,
knocked off the rum and then started the shoot.
I set her up in a few poses: "Yeah baby, that's it, cross your
legs, tilt your neck a little to the right. Yeah! Yeah! Work it
bitch! Sorry, I didn't mean to call you a bitch. Now,
I want you looking up - Things are falling from the sky -
Look at the things - Beautiful - Perfect - Unbutton your shirt -
Just the first button, don't worry - OH -Yeah - Yeah - I can
almost see your tits - Yes - That's it - Do the next button."
"John, you're not going to take pictures of me with my shirt
unbuttoned, sorry."
"Why? I won't show 'em to anybody, I promise!"
"Then what are you going to do with them?"
"I'll keep 'em for myself. For inspirational purposes. I'll look
at 'em before I go to sleep at night."
"Before you go to sleep?"
"Well, probably in the mornings too, you know, for
inspiration."
"Oh yeah, inspiration for what?"
"Baby, I'll compose gooey white sonnets and dedicate them
all to you."

I squeezed off two more shots before she left - definitely not
enough.
I picked up the phone again, punched another seven buttons,

got the Giant.

"Hey man, what are you doing?"
"Shit, what are you up to?"
"Nothing much man, sittin here with this camera. I need a
few pictures, think you can give me a hand?"
"Do I have to take my clothes off?"
"No, not at all, just come by and snap a couple photos of me.
It'll only take a few minutes."
"Are you going to take your clothes off?"
"No man, what's wrong with you?"
"Nothing, nothing, when should I come by?"
"Right now fucker."
"O.k. I'll be right over."

Whenever the Giant tells me 'I'll be right over', I know I've
got about 10 minutes before the ground starts shaking.

I run back to the store - more talls - same checkout girl and
when I get back to my place the Giant is already there - no
time to stroke -
Shit!

"Hey, you been waitin long?" I ask him
"Nah, only a little bit. So what's up? You want me to take
pictures of you?"
"Yeah, it should only take a few minutes. You want a beer?"
"Sure."

We worked on the beer, then, for the second time that day,
started the shoot.

"All right John, what kind of pictures are you looking for?
What's the theme here?"
"I don't really know."
"Well, what are you trying to say with these pictures?"
"I'm not sure. I just figured we'd snap away and see what
happens."
"O.k. let me think a minute."

He starts pacing the room. Shakes the whole building. Makes
a box with the thumb and index finger of both hands. Stares
through it. Adjusts the lights. Picks up the camera.

"O.k. put a cigarette in your mouth, look out the window -
very nice - now look at me, laugh at something - perfect -
now give me an angry face, angrier, get mad at the camera,
stop smiling damnit, imagine that the camera has just finished
screwing your mother, has just slapped her around the face
and ass with a belt . . . "
"Hey, why the fuck do you have to say the camera was
screwing my mother?"
"Perfect! That's the face. Scowl again. Yes! Now move over
by that piñata. Pick up that bowl. Start packing it."
"Like this?"
"Yeah, but look up at me. Lets get your face in it. Yes! Hey
. . . what's that on your arm?"
"Just a growth, don't worry about it."
"I'm not worried about it. Not at all. I want to use it. Yes!
That's it! Let's get that bastard on film. Pick your arm up,
turn your elbow, lower the chin, yes! Yes! What a photogenic
little fucker! Yes! More! That's it! Yes! That's fucken it!"

2 hours later,
we had run out of film. The beer was gone,
I was drunk
and the clock was ticking-
Somewhere in Dallas, a little boy scrapes his knee.
Giant squid,
beach themselves on La Jolla beach.
I wonder about that checkout girl
with her nice little ass and her nice little eyes and the radio
plays
The White Stripes
and after the song ends, 'This Protector' it's called - lots of
piano and good lyrics - I shut the thing off
open a can of tuna, and I figure I'll get the film developed
tomorrow morning

❧ ON THURSDAY NIGHT

I got in the place, sweating like mad (drip),
cursing the subway (shit),
stripping down to boxers (you fat
sexy bastard) while inhaling sixteen ounces
of the domestic beer.
Across 5 states
lay this 1 woman, and I pulled prick like some quick draw
shootist while thinking about round ass and brown hair and
I'm tugging cock and I'm still by the fridge and wind up
shooting white globs across kitchen tile as this genius type
idea
sparks up in my demented little brain.
I'm going to build a barge and sail to Ensenada.
I'm going to drop all assets (meager), secure lumber and oil
drums at rock bottom prices (stolen), and while I'm on this
barge (yellow Speedos and an eye patch), I'll write the
wildest,
drunkenest,
fucken novel that this slightly demented (did I say slightly?),
yet highly respected,
literary world
has ever seen.
And when (or if) I do get to Ensenada,
I'll buy 2
2 GODDAMNIT!
pearl-handled
.45's
and rob wetbacks
up and down the coast
for their pesos and their daughters and soon enough,
I'll have enough pesos,
and enough daughters, and the barge will be bursting
with currency and rotating,
leather-thonged
senoritas
while I type bad poetry

and ship it off
to you fuckers
for review. (Pause
for a commercial break from our sponsors this evening-
(This program has been brought to you by the good people at
Annheuser-Busche,
who would like to remind you,
that if you drink,
don't drive,
and if u do - then make sure ur eyes r closed, and that ur
hands r off the steering wheel, and that ur seatbelts
unfastened, and that u have at least 1 other degenerate to take
along for the ride so that when u hit the eternal flame
there's someone there
who gets ur jokes...

(sorry,
sorry,
that's the wrong message completely, don't do any of that
stupid shit, leave that to the real smart mothers
like myself
and of course,
Mr. Reilly, the poet who jumps out of moving cars while
giggling crazy,
and don't forget the Italian,
putting out the words,
faster,
and harder
then I screw with 2 blondes at 225 a piece and the bank
account reads
MONEY-MONEY-MONEY - John!
WHORES,
BOOZE,
LAUGHTER! Escape dream material so that you can write
your way out of the stock life and the stock women and speed
rack whiskey and sitting at some shitbox job that LSD
fed monkeys
could perform with the proper training and... (wait a minute,
how many levels did I just jump down? Shit. There should be
1,

2,
3
and with this bullshit
4
(and I'm playing very stupid games right now so here's 5)))))
And,
where did I leave off?
Fuck it!
Unsure,
but I drink faster than I type - 'So I shall return!' (yelling real
loud in an empty room)
after I replenish the ambrosia,
and in,
I'd say ten,
2 15 minutes, I'll be back on my personal
Mount Olympus,
tossing ridiculous thunderbolts,
with a mouth full of beer -

While I'm gone you should jack off or do laundry or think
about your parents -

Your half drunk,
red eyed,
and life stained captain -
john

☙ SELF INTERVIEW

John, in your writing there is a feel of animosity towards the
opposite sex. Would it be fair to call you a misogynist?

No, that's a bit extreme. It's true that in a few pieces I state
my distrust of women, but to be honest, I don't trust anybody.
Men, women, children, animals, some plants even, they all
swing equal weight. I try not to focus on any one group or sex
in particular.

So, you don't trust anybody - anybody at all?

No.

So, do you consider yourself to be paranoid?

No. Just smart.

Smart?

Yes, smart. Well, also experienced. Lets say that I'm smart and experienced. I like that.

So you feel that your animosity towards human, animal and plant kind is a result of intelligence and experience. Is that correct?

Yes ma'am.

Could you elaborate?

Of course I could.

Um . . . would you?

Well, look at this way; everybody in this world does what he or she does in order to fulfill a personal need or to accomplish a personal goal. Here's an example. The charity freaks organize fundraisers. They collect a few thousand dollars and feel like saints. That's not an easy feeling to come by. If it were, we'd see allot less of these guys on the street.

That's quite an interesting view.

Yeah it is. And I'd like you try something on your walk home one night. Give some change or a few dollars or whatever you can spare to the first bum you come across. See how it makes you feel. That charitable, I am good and I help others and I am looking out for my fellow man sensation, that's a high for these guys. They're nothing more than junkies. Glorified junkies. In the long run they do more to feed their own habit than they do to help others.

Hmmm. I think I'm beginning to see where you're coming from.

Good. But there's more. We also have religion pushers, and the religion pushers work to disseminate, no pun intended there, the Church or the Temple or the Mosque, or any of the others that I may have left out, in order to ensure their own social, political, mental and religious status within society. Now, dimwits aren't exactly drawing these conclusions. You get this from the philosophers and social scientists and the few underground knowledge freaks that make it their business to pick apart the world. These are all, uh, intellectual findings.

And the experience you were talking about?

Well, that's easy. Just by living life, I've come to believe that no one is safe from anything. Men, women, children, and animals have fucked me. Some plants even, and I've got scars and ripped shirts, chest pains, psychological issues, cracked mirrors and missing teeth to back me up on this. Men are thieves and women are murderers. Children are little monsters. The animals are mindless and a plant's sole concern is propagation - water and sun and nothing else. NOTHING ELSE. Hypothetical situation: Some planes are hijacked, and then, say, they're flown into the financial center of the world where your father just happens to work. Would the cactus show up to the funeral and shed tears? No. And neither would I nor would your furry gray kitten with the patch of white on his belly or half of the so-called friends you graduated from high school with. Sorry.

That's all right.

All the wheels will continue to turn. Purses will be snatched and bombs will be dropped. Television shows will air. Records will play without skipping a beat, and the maggots'll burrow through the rotten little channels of daddy's sweet corpse while smacking lips - oh so lovely.

Wow. That's certainly a mouthful.

Why, is that what you're looking for?

Excuse me?

Nothing, nothing, strike that comment.

Ok.

But do you see what I'm driving at?

I'm not sure.

Well, I veered off-course a bit, but to answer your question: No, I'm not a misogynist, it's just that I deal with allot of women and they've been a key source of inspiration for me. And if the women I deal with happen to be killers, then, shit, so be it, that's what gets bled onto the page. But understand, that off the page, the same animosity is felt for the entirety of the waking, walking, working, breathing, cancerous, luxury driven world. Bipeds, quadrupeds, plant matter, machines, co-workers, ex-girlfriends, current girlfriends, the grocer's wife, the stuck up women on the uptown A, that blond that shot me down last weekend at the bar when I offered to buy her a drink, that Asian I always walk past on West 3rd in the morning, my dyed brunette boss, the old Spanish lady that lives two doors down with her goddamned candles and smells of pot roast, those whores in Atlantic City, my 4th grade teacher, Ms. Greene, who had me suspended for sharpening my pencils and then jabbing the other kids during lunch time, the chick at the deli that refuses to sell me beer without an ID even though I'm there 4 days a week buying the same exact shit, the little Italian who works at the pizza joint and can never get my order right, Hillary Clinton, Dolly Parton, Cher, Brittany Spears, Christina Aguilera, the Victoria's Secret models and the secretary who had me fired for touching her ass on the elevator, which was an accident. So, no, I don't think it would be fair to call me a misogynist, not at all.

Oh, I see . . .

❧ PERSONALIZED BRUSH STROKES

Lava

blackened moments
and the hot struggle

'Scream at the mountains!'

and there's no answer from the landscape.

Time

ground-
grinded-
grinding
down to nothing, floats,
disappears
like smoke
and my fingers
look
yellow

these days,

they run on a movie reel
every now and then
the projectionist shows up
drunk,
runs the same reel
that was run the night before, sometimes
he runs it backwards
and it's something like
déjà vu
or
déjà senti - I'm
no longer sure, which one it is - I

just walk out of the theater,

'Yell at the beach!'
but there's no answer
from that landscape either.

I'm in the delicious middle

limbo

fence straddling half heart,
never a straight answer and always
the crooked smile, center of the room, stuck
between the floor and the ceiling.
Between the bird and the cat.
Between the fly
and the web
and a set
of 50 dollar
brown legs that I picked up last Wednesday - this stripper
type,
sits down
in the stool next to mine, reaches
red fingernails
down the front of her pants and pulls
a long,
curly hair
form her crotch - drops it
into my lap. I ask her what she's drinking, wave over the
bartender.
She works those 50 dollar legs - just the legs, they're all
that matters
when
they kick out and cross, fold over
one another, bend
at the knee and curve up
towards the hip - they

'Shout at the skies'
and of course,
there's no answer from the landscape - just cracks,
nicotine stains, a rusty hook and a brown
water mark
in the shape
of a rhinoceros - I'm wrapped up in sheets - Monday morning
death bed - white
overproofed

rum - July
29th, the year
is something crazy and I've
begun
to paint my own landscapes.

❦ TONIGHT

I'm burning midnight oil - down to the last beer,
in front of the machine,
the keyboard
swims up at me, reminds me I'm nobody, just another key -
John - you're just another key,
shit
you could be an M
or a T - that's it, you're a grain of sand - then, the mind
speaks up - we're all grains of sand, no more, You
don't mean a thing - then I speak up - I know, fuck! I know.
Hangman thoughts and swan dive psychology - Freud?
Anywhere? Psychiatrist in the house? Fuck it, I say - Tonight
I'm playing garage punk guitar riffs, down to the last chord,
the blonde
thinks I'm disgusting - John, when are you going to call the
doctor
about that thing on your arm - the Giant - I don't know man,
you said some
fucked up things
last time you were here,
shit - my sister - please, look, please, just change your shirt,
you really,
really
smell, I don't know what it is, but
its like,
like,
those smoking lounges at the airport terminal, a mix between
that
and the bathroom at the train station - Fuck it,

I say - Tonight
I'm going to lay down the

indes-

tructible line - open up my

ridiculous chest and let the blood
run across this page - 5 minutes ago,
I mixed this drink, now I'm on the

newly found,

white rum, mixed with this

berry cola, August 7th,
2thousandandtwo, my birthday
countdown
clock
hits zero
in exactly

seventeen days - I'll be
25
and I don't think I've
ever been more lost, than I am now - Fuck it,
I say Tonight
I'm banishing all thoughts of the future, all concern for the
consequences! -
throw Life
out the window - just keep moving
John, don't pay any attention
to those silly men with their butterfly nets - Fuck it,
I say - Tonight
I'm, I'm
I'm

. . . not sure . . . shit - I'm - Fuck it,
you know what,

figure it out for yourself . . .

❧ ON MY MIND

(Sittin on some wooden bench . . .

I've got a mug, Dewars and coke, listening
to more Frusciante guitar riffs,
I'm wearing pants,
too big for my waist,
the infamous Burroughs shirt, cigarette
sitting in my face. You know I'm thinking about you - right?
(I'm sure you are john) You've been on my mind
all day.

Woke up around twelve - and that's late for me - made some
eggs - showered and got high - you were on my mind.

About 5 I hit the liquor store - all this Dewars is getting
expensive - bottle of soda and a lime - I was thinking of you.

I got back to the place - message from this one blonde - called
her and told her to come by:

'I'm wearing a codpiece with your name on it baby! It's
bright yellow!'

- you were all over my mind.

The blonde came by - drank half my drink and smoked half
my shit -

Shit! -

finally got her in the bedroom - played jockey -

I was riding you.

About to come - tit in my mouth and she's moaning -
screamed out the wrong name -
and -

you ever see a rodeo -

just like that - I blew white load across bucking blonde and
she slapped my face -

I need to stop thinking about you.)

So now it's 9.

I've got this mug,
I'm on this wooden bench, the bottle is closing in on empty
and I was born in August. When were you born?
You ever been to New York?

Do you like strawberry ice-cream?

I do.

I also like fishing - you ever been fishing?

(What am I doing?) I need to piss. I need to make another
drink. The bugs are starting to come down and I will sacrifice
them all
in your name. See,
you're still on my mind. It's almost ten on some Saturday and
I feel that the cosmos are lining up. That tonight, is meant for
something - something BIG-
maybe I'll fight the bartender,
or maybe I'll set the place on fire by throwing a cigarette in
the trashcan, who knows . . .
Maybe
tonight,
I will do the undoable. (Which is?)
(I don't know, I don't think that far ahead - I just figured on
making the bar.) (That's a fine idea.)
(Yeah it is.) And I get undressed, jump in the shower, look
down

and

yeah . . .

I'm still thinking about you.

❧ SEND HOME THE SEARCH PARTY

let flies crawl
across rotten fruit

let lights sag
under the pressure of time

and my message to the press:

'Send home the search party,
I've found smooth eyes and
heavy breath
in the mirror thrill
of a hanging image.'

let tires roll
down rotten streets

let dust build
on the bookshelves of God,

and my message to the press:

'Send home the search party,
I've found slow life and
profound thought
in the water calm
of madman philosophy.'

'Send home the search party!'
let my rotten fingers
clutch at rotten dreams

'Send home the search party!'
and let my rotten dreams
slip through rotten fingers -

'Send home the search party!'

and my message to the press:

Please try back
at a later date,

right now
John
is nowhere
to be found.

∝ Sometimes, The Legs Won't Spread

I'm pissing at the urinal
I'm in aisle number three
I'm thinking about sailfish
I'm yelling into the phone

I'm on the cold,
easy beer, tonight, it's 75 degrees, I'm on some beach
the sand
feels good under my ass
and I'm writing these lines
while thinking:

Did Miller
ever argue with the ceiling
for more than thirty minutes?

Or Ernie,
did he ever trap a fly
under a glass and spend the afternoon
trying to make him cough up some information - 'Look
Pennilli - that uptown jewelry heist, give me a name or else
I'll beat it outa you.' That's me.
I'm playing the tough cop act and I announce this by saying
'I'm playing the tough cop act.'
'Bzzzzzt Bzzzzzt.' the fly says in agreement, he'll play
Pennilli, the tight-lipped gangster, got some Mafia
connections, is waiting on his lawyer.
I bring the spotlight in real close. Light a cigarette and tuck
thumbs into suspenders.
'So greaseball, you ready to start singing?'
'Bzzzzzt Bzzzzzt.' and Pennilli's one of those tough
customers, doesn't show any signs of cracking. I decide to

bring in some heavier persuasion, leeches maybe, or ticks,
when a middle-aged, female officer (Due to the lack of cast
members I will be playing this role as well. I announce this
by applying lipstick and saying 'I'm playing the middle-aged,
female officer act.' 'Bzzzzzt Bzzzzzt.' and
'Quiet on the set!'
'ACTION!')
walks into the interrogation room 'Looks like your lawyer
came through for you Pennilli.'
'Bzzzzzt Bzzzzzt, he always does copper - don't you guys get
that by now?'
(I wipe off the lipstick) 'Shut your mouth Pennilli.'
'What are you gonna do Bzzzzzt? Arrest me Bzzzzzt?'
'Arghhh, get this scum outa here.' (and
Cut!
Audience applause.
Cast takes a bow. and I -

doubt it . . .

I should keep my mind on the cold beer
and the 75 degrees
and just clutch
at these warm nights
and let the rest of the gang
take a stab at the literature.

☙ THE PHONE RINGS

and it's her, she tells me "I can't do my laundry! I rushed
home just so I could do it and now someone's using the
machine! Shit! I also think we need some time apart."

The phone rings and it's my mother, she asks "Do you want
anything from Istanbul? We landed yesterday and it's all so
beautiful! You know, you should really be here with your
brother and sister."

The phone rings and it's The Giant, he says "From now on

I'm calling you 'Pukes' - two nights in a row we drink and
two nights in a row you lose your shit - you're getting weak
man, WEAK - but you wanna make the bar later?"

The phone rings and it's a telemarketer
(I'm not buying)

The phone rings and it's a wrong number
(They're all wrong numbers)

The phone rings and it's some nut
breathing heavy
with a hand in his lap
and the phone rings

and the phone rings

and the people talk
and I wonder
if I should have the damned thing
disconnected

❧ SMARTEST CREATURES AROUND

I want the woman
who will kill me in under a month

And I like the songs
that make me forget my age

I hunt down these nights

that leave me broken and confused, half dressed
on Jersey sidewalk, dick wet, half cigarette
hanging
off dempsey lip . . .

I want the friends
who make deadly plans
involving pill shaped freedom
and 16 ounces
of The Escape Dream

And I like the bars
that are filled with dead eyed drunks and the speed rack
whiskey
runs two dollars a glass

I hunt down these nights

they leave me broken and confused, black eyed
on Manhattan street, right canine
chipped to shit, with that same half cigarette
hanging
off dempsey lip . . .

Us humans
(HA!)
Smartest creatures around,
isn't that right?

❧ THE PROCESS

it starts like some
starched
white
business shirt

and then

brain,
fingers,
gut,

GUT! begins to spit these,
these
unidentifiable
fucking objects and they come crawling
at an insectile, machine gun type pace,
fast, unpredictable, crashing against one another or ganging
up, forming groups, and these ones in groups, these strong
armed bastards, they look up at me from that starched white
shirt, they give me sneers

of violent
suspicion,
they're on the edge of revolt and they ask 'Now what exactly
is all this shit worth?'

and it ends,
with me
and the man upstairs,
and we're in our respective corners,
and we're in our bloodied shirts,
and we're both laughing
because we know the punch line
to that old joke

ॐ WRITING AT 45 MILES AN HOUR

3 tons - rickety
pickup truck w/ 2 pints of ambrosia soaring sweet thru my
brains and there's more in the back seat - cardboard box
winks real pretty in the rearview - and I make a stop to deal
w/ this guy -
some real special
blueberry buds and maybe I shouldn't be writing at 45 miles
an hour but
when the words command
the writer obeys . . . (Who's the writer? Not sure. Is there a
writer in the house? Anywhere?)

3 tons - rickety
pickup truck w/ 2 bowls of blueberry buzzing heavy thru my
brains and another four grams hidden behind the face of the
steering wheel - I pull out pint #3 and giggle rotten through a
stop sign and maybe I shouldn't be writing at 45 miles an
hour but
when the words command
the writer yells . . . (Wait a minute, who's the writer? Not
sure. Is there a writer in the house? No, but I like yelling, so
screw it, I'll be the writer!) And I yell: No Stop Signs! No

Red Lights!
Keep Moving! Death
is Standing Still! Death
is the Final Red Light! The Ultimate Stop Sign! Keep
Fucking
Moving!

3 tons - rickety
pickup truck w/ 2 police cruisers flashing hot for my ass and
the cigarette juts out from my face, spills ashes
across my lap and I'm smiling pretty, scribbling these
demented little lines and maybe
I shouldn't be writing at 45 miles an hour but
if I didn't
then
what else would you fuckers be reading right now?

❦ TUESDAY AT THE BOWERY

I had been harassing this redhead in my office for three
months, and every time I asked her out, she turned me down.
It was a Tuesday when she finally accepted and I was thrown
off guard. I suggested a bar in the neighborhood, that I had
never been to, and we made happy hour.

At the time I was drinking in the Astoria bars, where draft
beer was under two dollars and the speed rack cocktails sold
for three. We got in this West Village place and it was five-
dollar drafts, my Dewars ran seven and change - Shit! But it
was only the third of the month; my bank account read 1800
and the redhead looked good.

We took a table in the back and
started on
the drinks.

The place started filling up; couples here and there, making
the after work, 'how was your day' conversation, while
sucking up the expensive drinks, a few stragglers in business

suits and groups of young men with salon style haircuts. At the table, I sat with the redhead, telling barroom jokes.

Time moved while we laughed.

Soon I noticed the couples leaving. Only the stragglers and salon types remained and a new bartender had taken control. More salon types walked in, groups at a time and some were holding hands. I was into the fourth drink, scotch-whiskey with soda, and I thought nothing of it. Manhattan, no, wait, the Village, especially in the spring, which it now was, is the East coast epicenter of homosexuality. The outdoor cafés and restaurants surrounding Washington Square Park become infested by espresso sipping queens with plucked eyebrows. They wear Capri pants and talk on cellular phones.

Stylish men,
with
well-
maintained hair and
manicured nails,
were all part of
the normal scene.

Some are execs and they sit in designer suits. They scan the headlines of The Wall Street Journal or some other business rag while punching lunch dates into their electronic organizers.

So,
like I said,
I thought nothing of it.
I knocked off my drink and told the redhead that I was going to the bathroom. Since this was my first time in the place I walked over to the bartender and asked him where it was. He pointed at a set of doors and gave me a wolf's smile. I also believe that he winked at me.

There was a wait for the bathroom; two salon boys stood in front of me; they talked and I listened:

Salon Boy 1: "This place is simply dazzling! When I first started coming here you couldn't find more than ten fairies on a Tuesday night, now look at it; wall to wall males - Dazzling!"

Salon Boy 2: "You're soooo right Eric. Do you remember when it was just Willie and a few of the uptown boys in here? That sure got old."

Salon Boy 1: "Yeah it did, but now there's cock everywhere! I can't remember the last time I left this place alone!"

Salon Boy 2: "Me either!"

Then Salon Boy 1 was up to bat and I was standing with number 2.

John: "Hey let me ask you a question - is this some, uh, special bar or something?"

Salon Boy 2: "Do you mean is it a gay bar?

John: "Yeah, I didn't wanna be rude or anything."

Salon Boy 2: "It's o.k. But to answer your question - no, it's a regular bar, but Tuesday is gay night."

John: "Oh . . . I didn't know that, first time in the place."

Then it was number 2's turn. I waited a few more minutes, and when a young, gelled, and styled Latino came out, it was my turn.

The bathroom was packed. Salon Boy 1 sat on the counter smoking a joint; he took a deep pull, and then handed it to another boy. There were three stalls along the north wall and a string of urinals stood opposite. The stall doors were closed but a gap between the floor and the bottom of the doors showed me two sets of legs. The third stall emitted some very sloppy and wet noises. I noted one set of legs and one set of knees in that third stall.

Nobody was using the bathroom; they were all just hanging out in there. No wonder there was a wait! I walked over to one of the urinals, stood about six inches from the porcelain, unzipped, and let it go.

One Mary was on my left. He kept licking at his lips and I

could tell he was getting excited. He walked over, stood next to me, and peered into the urinal.

The Mary: "Ooooh, looks like we have a stud here boys."

The Boys: "Ooooh. How big is he Stevie? Is he circumcised? Hmmm."

Then Salon Boy 2 peeks out from over the top of one of the stalls.

Salon Boy 2: "Oh this is his first night. Be gentle with him Stevie!"

Stevie/The Mary: "A first timer huh. Well, first timer, how'd you like to take a ride with a real veteran? Show you all the ropes."

(And I'd heard the stories. Roving gangs of homosexuals attacking straights; beating and subjecting them to acts of buggery.)

John: "Sorry Stevie boy, but my old man would just about kill me, maybe another time."

I finished up, zipped up, and walked out of the bathroom.
I didn't stop to wash my hands.

Of all the places!
Of all the nights!
Why?
Why'd I pick THIS particular place on THIS particular night?
- Shit!

On my way back to the table I stopped at the bar, called for my scotch-whiskey with soda and an imported beer for the redhead. The bartender brought the drinks out and flashed that wolf-smile again. I started to pull bills from my pocket and he told me not to worry, this round was on the house. Thanks Wolf -

I got to the table and the redhead was smoking a cigarette, her legs crossed, and her beer empty. She looked upset.

Redhead: "What took you so long?"

John: "There was a line for the bathroom and then I stopped for drinks. I got you another beer."

Redhead: "Thanks. Hey, did you notice that there isn't a single woman in this place besides me?"

John: "Yeah, I was talking to some fellows while waiting, they told me that Tuesday is gay night."

Redhead: "I knew it! There's nothing but a bunch of dirty fags in here."

John: "Oh come on, they're not that bad. I just got these drinks for free."

Redhead: "So what if you got free drinks! That doesn't change the fact that we're in a gay bar."

John: "Look, it's not a GAY bar, they just have a GAY night. Let's see if we can get more free drinks."

Redhead: "No way, I don't even want this beer; it's all, all gayed up, this whole place is gayed up, lets get the fuck outa here."
And she stood up, put on coat, slung purse over shoulder and looked at me.

John: "Well, I plan on finishing my drink. You sure you don't want your beer?"

Redhead: "No I just wanna leave."

John: "Why, what's the big deal?"

Redhead: "I hate fags! That's the big deal!"

John: "Serious . . . Well, I think they're alright people. Just as long as no one invades my space, I don't really care. Look why don't you finish your beer and then we'll take off."

Redhead: "No! I wanna leave now."

John: "Well I'm not leaving till I finish this drink."

She glared at me while I thought:

This girl is completely fucken ridiculous.
But - maybe her father was gay,

maybe he ran out on her and her mother when she was three, left them to starve while he toured the French Riviera.
Maybe,
but I doubt it, besides I'm not leaving two full drinks, no way!
In another week or so I'd be dead broke, I'd be counting change to buy domestic beer and smoking butts from the ashtray.

I finished my Dewars and picked up her beer.

Redhead: "Are you fucking kidding me? Didn't I just tell you that I wanted to leave?"

John: "Yeah you told me, but like I said before - I'm finishing these drinks before I go anywhere."

Redhead: "You know what, I always thought there was something queer about you, but now I'm certain."

John: "Oh yeah, and what are you certain about?"

Redhead: "Well, why else would you bring me to this dirty fag place? It's because you're a dirty fag yourself, that's why!" She stormed towards the door, grabbed the handle, then turned around -

Redhead: "And I'm gonna tell everybody in the office tomorrow!"

I lifted that imported beer and pulled hard. It was delicious! Really, a very classy tasting beer and as soon as I finished off the bottle I headed back for another. The Wolf saw me coming and by the time I reached the bar he had my order ready, the wolf-smile was plastered across his face and I wasn't surprised when he told me that this round, just like the last, was also on the house.
Thanks again Wolf -

There was an open stool at the end of the bar and I sat down with my two free drinks. I lit a cigarette and looked around. This place was just hopping with homosexuality. There was a lounge area with couches. Men sat with their legs draped across each other, some blew kisses across the room and they all drank cosmopolitans. Next to me two guys were blowing bubbles into their drinks and giggling. I drained the scotch-whiskey and started on the beer. The Wolf automatically came with the refill, set it down in front of me, and leaned on his elbows.

The Wolf: "Looks like you're on some type of mission."

John: "Excuse me?"

The Wolf: "The way you're drinking. It's like you have to meet a quota or something."

John: "Oh, yeah. I guess you can say that."

The Wolf: "Well, if you keep it up I'm gonna have to start charging you."

(He said this while batting the eyelashes.)
(I batted mine right back.)

John: "Now, you wouldn't do that to meeee, would you?"

The Wolf: "Nah, I don't think I could. You're just toooo cute!"
(He flashed wolf-teeth.)
(While I downed the beer.)

John: "Well then keep em coming!"

The Wolf: "By the way, I'm Mike."
(He holds out his hand.)
(And I shake.)

John: "Nice to meet ya Mike, name's John."

Mike/The Wolf: "So John, you ready for another round?"

John: "Always Mike, always!"

Mike/The Wolf winks and goes for the refill, he brings the two drinks over and I start making them disappear.

Mike/The Wolf: "So, John, are you here alone tonight?"

John: "Well, I was with this horrid girl, simply horrid, but then she left."

Mike/The Wolf: "Poor, poor John."

John: "Tell me about it, these women just don't care Mike - they're horrid!"

Mike/The Wolf: "Oh don't be so down. If you wait till my shift is over you can come home with me. Maybe it'll cheer you up"

John: "I'd love to, but my old man would kill me."

Mike/The Wolf: "Who says he has to know?"

John: "You don't understand Mike, he's a madman. When I come home at night he sniffs at my balls and ass and if there's even a hint of come he'll beat the hell out of me."

Mike/The Wolf: "That's terrible!"

John: "I know, I know."

Mike/The Wolf: "You should get away from him before he hurts you."

John: "I wish I could Mike, I really wish I could."
(He gives me an appraising look.)
(I put on the hurt little boy face and sigh.)

Mike/The Wolf: "Just a second, I'll be right back."

Mike/The Wolf walks over to a tall Spaniard and talks with him. He gestures at me with his eyes and I nod in recognition. They talk for a few minutes and then he comes back.

Mike/The Wolf: "I just talked to my roommate Federico, he says you can stay with us if you want."

John: "That's real nice of you Mike, but I just couldn't do it."

Mike/The Wolf: "How come? Wait, I know, you love him don't you?"

John: "Yeah that's the problem. That's always the problem."

(I smile, real sheepishly, and shrug my shoulders.)
(He reaches over the bar and strokes my head.)

Mike/The Wolf: "Poor, poor John."

John: "I know Mike, it's just killing me. Killing me I tell you!"

Mike/The Wolf: "Oh John. Poor John. Here have another drink."

John: "Thank you Mike, you know, you're a real, Grade A gentleman."

I milked Mike/The Wolf till 2 am and caught the N train to Astoria. I carried high blood alcohol content, stumbled to my apartment, dropped my key twice before fitting it into the lock, then finally managed to get inside. In the fridge lay the carcass of a twelve pack I had brought down the night before, and I, playing the scavenger role, jumped at the remains. I rolled a small joint and turned on the radio, sat down on the couch with the beer, thinking:

It's the little tricks that really help you get by.

○ WHO WANTS SOME

some (cock) - cock and bull sad song when it rains stumbling down some side street looking for sweetheart or the right music or the right drink and I'm thinking sisyphus and that leads to camus philosophy in some dark room with the walls caved in round squeaky pipes exposed and there's some hair and legs the outline of a torso behind the glass shower screen and I don't hear no breathing momma which means packed bags and who wants to put up with some drunk for a few weeks even if he promises it's just till he gets back on his feet then he'll repay you with cash made off some simple trade of abused mind for signed paycheck and that translates at a light speed into some empty bottles and half-death-death bed looking up at you with some swollen eyes and there's this real tired sounding voice it's presence announced by some corpse breath and its simply asking:

who wants some?

CR GRATITUDE IN NEVADA

clock reads 841
cigarette in my mouth
10th floor
of the San Remo Hotel, brown bottle
sits in my fist
and I take a pull;

flat, warm, but right now
it doesn't matter - the woman
is in bed,
there're cards
downstairs, 300 dollars
in my right front pocket
and a 24 hr bar, with my name
carved into the mahogany - viva
Las Vegas I
feel
so good -

in the elevator, button pushed, floating down, ground floor
early morning and across my chest
the Chinaski t-shirt, in bright
orange letters
it reads 'Fuck You' and I gotta say:

thank you Hank,
for
holding the door.

CR BAR AT THE SANREMOHOTEL

i have to say-
that this is my first time, sitting in a bar
and writing my shit.

usually,

the process

is performed in solitude, usually
in front of 'the machine'
with the music
loud
and the eyes
red - but today,
one hundred
and 11 degrees, middle of the
nevada desert, i suck down dewars and coke
at four bucks a glass
and scribble these thoughts
on beautiful
bar
napkins -

is it too early to drink like this? - no,
not at all john. this is vegas and you're not the only one at the
bar - put em away
and then hit the tables - it's so

easy to gamble
w/ this much liquor in the system - the dreams
blow up in the head - one drink down
and i think i'm a winner, 2 drinks down
and i know i am . . . by the 5th drink,
cockeyed, cocky, the clock reads 9thirty, and there's a
small fortune
crawling
towards my
unsteady hands.

⌘ Bar At The Sanremohotel2

bartender just came by to freshen the drink, what's that
you're writing young man?
and I tell her I'm a journalist.
you sure don't look like a journalist,

maybe it's the buck shirt, maybe it's all the glasses I've
emptied, who knows? I shrug the shoulders.
well, which paper do you write for?
the cat house gazette, I tell her, it's an electronic publication.
I travel all over the states, finding underground bordellos,
sniffing out the sex shops, peeking up skirts, you know, all
the usual.
she walks away, at the end of the bar sits some broken down
blonde number, the face says 45, but the body screams
TWENTY, perky, curvy and she flashes a showgirl's smile - I
can have her, that's what the smile tells me, I can lay her
down and she'd admit me,
I keep looking, reading into the smile and I read deeper -
I have two kids at home
and no husband
and the rent is late
and you look like a fuck-up but I bet you could make some of
the problems go away and - shit - I drain the 6th drink, of
Tuesday morning
and walk away -

I wouldn't have been any good for her, besides, I'm better off
at the tables,
at least there,
I'm the one getting fucked
and there's no
awkward conversation
to deal with in the morning

⌘ TYPE

ing -
here, now, burroughs t-shirt and double vision and I spent the
night at sequoias on the water with maria because she came
by the 2 dollar place and kissed me like I was last man
standing and I swear
this has nothing

to do w/ my cock.

On the walk from the 2 dollar place:

I call her brown eyes and she says 'I've never met anyone
like u before.
Sometimes,
I think ur crazy, certifiable,
and sometimes
I just want to hug you - does that make any sense?' and I
laugh
because maria, my heart pumps ridiculous, putrid, piss and
puss and every dirty
infectious
drop
is engineered
special
and just
for you, and yes, it does make sense, and yes,
I do understand, and baby,
I want to tell u a story -
about my father and mother, about how they knew/loved each
other since they were 5 yrs old, about how one shipped off to
war
and one
moved to california
and how after the war, one came back and then flew to
california and asked for the other one's hand and that when I
look at you, ah

fuck

maria . . .

y'd I walk outa the place while u were dancing with some
prick? And y am I sitting here
typing all this trash when I can have ur legs rapped round my
neck?

And y didn't I call my good friend Grella at 8 like I told him I
would? And by the way,

what are you doing tomorrow night?

Ridiculous

horrible
shit -

and at seqoias (spelling?) some club kid walks over and asks

'you john dempsey?'

'john who?'

'dempsey, john dempsey?'

'nah man, wrong person.' while I'm sucking dewars with
coke and watching maria dance,

and she moves in just this way -

makes my butter ass melt.

CR WHAT DID YOU THINK

That I just threw in the towel,
stepped outa the ring and
called it
quits?

Huh?

Shit,

of course not - (but you know,
maybe you should think about taking a little break) (never)
Baby,

I'm in LA, (no you're not) I'm writing sitcoms and lying
around with the heavy nosed blondes (now that, wouldn't
surprise me) I'm at the pool (you mean your bathtub) with the
AM beer (12 bucks a case) and the expensive
sun
glasses (maaan,
that's just duct tape and plastic wrap
colored in

with a black marker -

you're losing your grip john).

O.k.
how about this:

I've been real busy,
working on something big - bigger than the usual. Bigger
than

all my other

pink little

poems, bigger even

than my SELF (and y wasn't I informed about all this?)
(because ur input wasn't needed) (but what is it exactly?
what's this BIG THING all about?) (I can't tell you that)
(how come?)
(I just can't . . .)

And it's tough,
fighting this personal
uphill
battle where
just about every one/thing is the enemy -

the lovers,
the friends and the mind - that most dangerous
of all bitches - and the clock and the television and the
disobedient, undisciplined, brink of
revolution
type fingers that type only
what makes THEM happy ((like this)) and barbecues with
lots to drink and the hashinated keif at 50 bucks a gram (new
york price) that knocks me on my ass and leaves me with no
thoughts of finishing the book. (wait a minute - did you just
say book?) (no,
slip of the tongue, pay no attention to that) (but I distinctly
heard you say) (shut the fuck up man) But today,
today is different, today is literary back flips and another
chapter marching steadily down the page like some high

stepping army. Today,
I look over 4 days of binge writing, all the words
dripping with a mixture of madness, medication, alcohol (and
pretension - don't forget that you ego driven bastard)
philosophy, sex
and
violence. The style screams 'Dempsey!' right in your face
and makes you want to reach down into your crotch with
eager fingers and nipples
at the ready, that first wave of orgasm
dancing a wet jig
behind your intently
reading
eyes . . .

What did you think? That I'd disappear that easy, that I'd just
vanish off the scene
without dropping
the BIG COMMUNICATION? (Never - I'm already
coming back into view)

What did you think? That I'd peter and sputter out like some
engine that's been fed nitrous methanol for a quarter of a
century and then one day the tank reads an inflexible empty?
(Think again-
I've just
upgraded to rocket fuel, an experimental mixture
of hydrogen
and helium
and it drives through my system like some berserk speedball
charging every cell with enough energy for me to end this
damned thing in just the way that it should . . .)

Your degenerate
and cockeyed
correspondent from the edge - john

CR TYPE IT

So Maria called it quits with me because I didn't love her
enough or because I didn't know how to love or because I
would pull 3-day
disappearing acts and show up on her doorstep
with scratch marks

across

my back.

(The phone rings and I answer and it's her voice.

She tells me all of this
and then I type it.)

And I fell for Maria,
no questions asked: I called her Brown-Eyes and she told me
that I was nuts and we drank
under the lights
of downtown Manhattan while the world

moved

around us.

(I'm still on the phone and I'm listening to her talk.
She says,

"John,
I'm sorry,
I never meant to hurt you
or for it to turn out like this."

and I type it.)

This year alone:
I've lost 2 blondes, a little Italian, 3 jobs, 4 friends, and now,

Maria. (Last year was even worse
and I think about that,

and then I type it: Last year was even worse.

Last year
I lost 4 blondes, one
half Mexican, 5 friends
and I couldn't even get a job,
let alone lose one.)

And there's a grinding,
somewhere between my stomach and my chest (that's
Maria's place)

and I listen to Bob Marley
while smoking my long joints
while drinking my lonely beer
and I should know by now,
to never bet on the women, but with Maria,

I just couldn't help it, and I couldn't help being myself and
maybe that's the reason
for all these women who slam the door, maybe I'm too much
myself and maybe that's why I can't hold jobs and the cause
for my friends
to fade out of the picture
and sail off
on some ship
while I
tread water and

type

it.

∝ THE SUNDAY MORNING DEMPSEY HOUR

Yellow

Hello? John?

Sorry, no John here, wrong number.

Oh, come on John.

On what?

What?

On you, that's what.

Me?

Yeah you, all over your face and your tits! Yeah, you're such a dirty little . . .

John - what the fuck is wrong with you!

Sorry, sorry. I got sidetracked for a minute, what's up baby?

Well, I was going to ask you if you wanted to come to the beach with me, but I'm not so sure anymore.

Yeah, yeah! The beach! When are we leaving?

I'll be there in 20 minutes. Start getting ready.

O.k. I'm gonna wear my new bathing suit. It's made entirely out of leather.

Bye John.

Can we collect jellyfish?

Bye John.

I wanna catch crabs!

Bye John.

I wanna finger a starfish!

It was Sunday morning. Her car pulled up at 10:30 and the law said no beer before twelve. Shit! That meant we'd have to buy beer at the beach. And that's expensive. Something like 5 bucks a glass. More shit!

But I did have half a joint. We smoked that while navigating the parkways.

Eventually, we made the beach. Parked the car, hopped out, collected beach chairs and beach towels, hit the sand, walked 5 minutes, and planted our asses. The sun was high, our eyes were red and a steady breeze was coming in from the east. I shoved a cigarette into one of the holes of my face, started humming, feeling good - I've always liked the beach.

She was staring at a magazine: People - her blue eyes fixed,
reading some story about rescuing miners.

I was staring at the crowd: People - my brown eyes fixed,
thinking up some story about how this giant
Chinese
Snakehead Fish was gonna come up out of the water with
sharp teeth gleaming and little children screaming and the
thing is ten feet long, weighs half a ton, has this insatiable
appetite and the whole crowd is frozen, parents
watch sons and daughters disappear between the fish's jaws
and then,
from out of nowhere, just as the fish is bearing down on some
hot number in a blue
string bikini, I would jump onto the scene, carrying spear, I
would run at the fish, knock the bikini out of the way, launch
myself up, 5 feet off the ground, position the spear so that it
would come down, hard, through the fish eye, and my aim is
good, direct hit, and then the spear punches through cartilage,
punctures the fish brain and I land, straddling the fish body
while it tosses in the waves and as I give the spear a twist, it
would make this death shriek and with a final spasm it would
toss me over it's head before crashing onto it's side, blood
and membrane dribbling from the spear handle, and I'd get up
out of the water, real nonchalant like and the whole beach
would be clapping and yelling bravo, our hero and the blue
bikini would walk up, dreamy, bedroom eyes, and then she'd
stick her tongue, deep, into my mouth while breathing real
heavy and her breasts pushing into me and I could feel the
heat, coming off her crotch and . . .

I was getting a hard on. I turned to the woman and told her
the story, leaving out the blue bikini part. She listened and
when I was finished:

You would never do that John. You'd be too scared to fight
the fish. I know you - you're no hero.

Well, I think I'd be a fine hero, maybe. Who cares, lets go
down to the water.

We weaved through the clumps of beach people. They were

lying on towels and they were shaped like fruit. Some looked like plums. Others looked like bananas. The babies were grapes and the elderly were prunes - fruit salad on the sand.

A few had radios but they were all tuned to bad stations. A few of them drank beer and that made me think of the time. Was it past twelve yet?

Shit!

We got down to the water. The waves crashed at our feet and strings of greenish, brown seaweed floated in the surf. We waded out past the breakers. I saw grapes. They were lying on boogie boards and smiling, talking, waiting on the next wave and kicking their grape feet.

Don't they look like grapes? (I asked her)

Who?

Those little kids, the ones on boogie boards. Don't they look just like little grapes?

No John, they look just like little kids.

Oh. Well what about that old guy over there. Doesn't he look like a prune?

What old guy?

That old guy. (I said pointing towards the sand)

Where?

Ah, forget it. Hey, you think it's twelve o'clock yet?

Probably.

O.k. I'll race you back. Loser buys first round.

She had taken a lifeguard course - a strong swimmer. I've got an open water diver's license - also a strong swimmer. We dove into the waves and hauled ass for the shore. She had me by a few feet and as we closed in on the beach, I reached out, grabbed her by the ankle, and pulled back.

It's a tie! (I said getting out of the water)

No it wasn't, you cheated. You can't even beat a girl without cheating. That's pitiful.

What are you talking about? I didn't cheat.

Oh yeah, then who pulled my leg?

I don't know, maybe it was the Snakehead Fish!

Yeah, I'm sure that's what it was John.

Back to the chairs, dried off, lit another cigarette, walked towards the concession stand. On the way, I saw two seagulls. They were fighting over a brown paper bag and I told her the bag was filled with dog's ears.

I swear! I saw one sticking out from the top of the bag, looked like it came from a German Shepard!

Whatever John.

We ordered four beers and sat down at one of the wooden benches. We drank the four, ordered another two, and got back to the chairs. The sun had moved 30 degrees along its arc and we had to shift the chairs. Did that, and then replanted our asses. A well-built blonde walked by and I pretended not to see her. Then a well-built brunette walked by and I pretended not to see her either. I sucked down my beer and started pulling on a loose string from my boxer shorts. For some reason, I always wore boxer shorts under my swim trunks. I kept pulling, and the string kept coming, and after five minutes, I had managed to remove the entire elastic band of my shorts. John, what are you doing?

I don't know. What are you doing?

Watching you.

Oh. Is it past twelve yet?

You know it's past twelve. Don't play these little games with me.

And then my beer was finished. She had barely touched her own. Beads of condensation rolled down the sides of the glass and all that beer looked like golden water and my thirst was like something tangible. Like the sand, or a Frisbee - I could almost see my thirst, I thought that if I looked hard enough, I would be able to make out an image, I strained my eyes, looking down towards my stomach, expecting something to happen, anything and when nothing happened, I drank her beer.

John!

Don't worry, I'll get you another.

She didn't want to walk back. I went alone. Back past the seagulls, past the fruit, feet on the hot sand, and a sensation of sliding cotton around my waist. Shit! The boxer shorts, short of the elastic band, were making their way down my hips. Some of the cloth stuck out from the bottom of my swim trunks. Some of the fruits looked at me and I started to sweat. I reached a hand down the back of my trunks and tried to adjust the boxers. I had my hand in my ass when two melons walked by - big, blue ribbon melons. They looked like they were being fed growth hormones. Anabolic Miracle-Grow! One of the melons smiled, opened his fruit mouth.

What are you doing you pervert?

Looking for your mother's wedding ring. What the hell are you doing Fruit?

What was that?

You heard me Fruit. I'm looking for your mother's...

He brought the right to my chin. I dropped to the sand; hand in my ass, still trying to fix the shorts. The two fruits laughed and their chests jiggled and their muscles bounced and with a final call 'You fucken perv' walked away. I rolled onto my stomach. Pulled my hand out of my ass, got to my feet and went back to walking. By the time I got to the concession stand the shorts were back down and sticking out of my trunks. Shit!

I went into the bathroom, took the shorts off, threw them in the trash. I looked in the mirror; saw a spot of purple on my face, smiled. Beautiful! You're fucken beautiful baby!

Washed my hands, walked out, got on line, got the beer and walked back down the beach. Made it without incident, and got into the chair.

Hey, what's that on your face?

Some melon punched me.

A melon?

Yeah and then the fruit stole my shorts.

Your shorts? A fruit?

Yeah, can you believe it? This whole beach is nuts. Fruits and nuts - Nuts and fruits. There's no escape.

Wait, John, can't you just tell me what happened?

I just did, I was walking along and then some melon . . .

What the fuck do you mean 'some melon'?

A fruit.

Like a fag?

Well, he did steal my boxers.

I don't think anyone would steal your boxers. You were probably being a wiseass and you mouthed off to the wrong person.

Not at all, the fruit called me a pervert and then pocketed me knickers.

I swear to god John!

What? What? I didn't do a thing.

I'm sure you didn't. Every time we go somewhere, something happens. You just can't stay out of trouble.

It really wasn't my fault. Honest to god.

Whatever John. And pull your trunks up; half the beach can see your ass! (I pulled my trunks up)

Is that better?

Yes. Thank you. Now, do you think we can have a nice, normal time?

Yeah, why not baby?

Oooooh! You know why not. You're always getting into something or starting something. I just want to relax for once.

O.k. I'll be good.

Good.

We drank the beer and let the sun cook our skin. My face hurt. I smoked two cigarettes, kept my mouth shut and soon it was time to leave. We threw out the empty glasses, brushed sand off the towels, folded chairs and walked back to the car. Got in, started the thing, put it into gear, and started moving. Silence, until we made the parkway.

You know what John?

What honey?

Sometimes, I really wish that a video camera would follow you around and record all the crazy things you say and all the shit that you get into.

Hey, I like that idea. It would probably make a hit TV Show! I could be famous! Lets go to NBC! Right now!

No, no John. Not for a show, but so that you can watch it and then maybe after seeing it you'll realize that . . .

No damnit! Realize nothing! Shit and piss! NBC! I even have a name for it. We'll call it The Sunday Morning Dempsey Hour!

Ah fuck, I can't even have a normal conversation with you.

Of course you can honey. But this idea of yours! Shit! It's a gem I tell you - a gem damnit!

And just then this car pulled next to us. The driver had a head like an antelope and I was thinking about The Sunday Morning Dempsey Hour. NBC! Hollywood! Shit! I rolled down my window, stuck my head out, opened my mouth and . . .

CR COLLABORATING WITH AN ARAB

I'm sitting here

writing this, now, what is it exactly that I'm writing?
not sure - but as that dash hits the screen there's a knock at
my door,

and I know who it is by the knock - 2 short - a pause - 3 short

it's the Arab next door and I yell:

come on in.

what you doin man?

typin, what about you?

shit, shit - what you typin?

everything man, everything!

serious . . . everything huh, sounds interesting.

yeah man, it's dynamic, top of the line, cutting edge shit here.

the Arab carries a paper bag, it's raining outside and the bag
is falling apart, I can see the outline of a box, my senses let
me know - domestic beer and I tell him

sit your ass down.

ahhh . . . so man, what else u been up to?

the same old, grinding away at the grind, typing away at the
typer.

yeah, I hear that shit all the time - clickety clack - clackety
click - my girlfriend asked me what it was the other day and I
told her that you have this electro-magnetic masturbation suit,
shoots stimulus waves at your cock and ass, the noises are
metering equipment that tick off levels of voltage in relation
to orgasmic effect - you want a beer?

masturbation suit huh, yeah I'll take one, so what did she say?

she got real hot over the whole thing, started squirming

around in her seat, she wanted to come here and see it, when I told her it was out of the question, she told me to describe it to her again, she got twice as hot, best ass I've had in two years!

that sounds good man, real good.

it was man, like I said, best in two years, but hey, let me ask you something.

what's that?

are you really typing everything, for instance, are you typing about bullfights?

actually, no - no bullfights, but, there is a story where the main character meets a young boy who dreams of breeding these fighting horses, he lives on a ranch with his father and he's got this special type horse trained to charge the cape, fights with a wooden sword, has this little dog running all over the place, really touching shit.

hmmm, interesting, what about fishing, everyone loves a good fishing story!

nah, no fishing stories right now.

love story?

nope, no love stories.

comedy?

well, in a way, yes, just haven't written it yet, you see it's about this one time I was with the giant, you know who I'm talking about right?

yeah that real big fucker that comes by here.

yeah him.

you know, at first, I thought you two were queer for each other.

what the fuck - why would you think that?

I don't know, all that giggling and shit you guys are always doing, just struck me as queer.

oh, well for the record, we're not queer, can I finish up now?

yeah, of course, want another beer?

yeah, so this comedy, its about this one time with the giant, he had just driven home from Florida and during one of his pit stops he bought a piñata -

a piñata, what's that?

you know, papier-mâché dolls and animals and shit, you fill them with candy then blindfold children -

wait a minute, why are you blindfolding children, what did they do?

man the children didn't do anything, its all part of the piñata deal.

oh, ok, continue.

well, you blindfold the children -

hold up, are any of these children afraid of the dark?

shit, it doesn't matter, forget the children, there's no children at all, lets say its grown men and they're blindfolded, how's that?

that's better, man when I was younger I was terrified of the dark, terrified!

you know what, fuck this whole explanation, I don't even have a comedy story.

oh, so then you're really not writing about everything, are you?

nah, I guess not.

well, you mind if I give it a shot?

shit, go right ahead mother, mind if I grab another beer?

not at all man.

and the Arab sits at the typer, screws up his eyebrows and jumps at it

(this is me, the Arab typing, hello fuckers! I'm not sure what
to write but I hear John at this goddamn thing all the time and
think: shit, I can type too, I've got stories, like once I was
walking around Cairo, it was about one in the morning, and in
Egypt, when the sun goes down it gets real fucken cold, what
you see on the street after sunset is quite the scene, packs of
stray dogs rule the night with rabid dog grins, attack any
passerby without discretion, and when the big freeze comes
down on them, the dogs adapt in such a cunning way that it
amazes the first time viewer, what they do is hunt out
recently parked cars, climb atop the hoods, and lay down in
groups so as to absorb the heat coming off a still warm
engine, really smart fuckers those dogs, but that's not the
story, just a side note of interest, the story is that I saw this
one character, male, couldn't of been more than 12, riding a
donkey, and this kid was in rags, dirt clung to him in patches
and dust came off him when the wind blew, even the donkey
was in bad shape and looking half dead from starvation, and
as I passed him on the street a queer beeping noise was
emitted from his person, and this ragged, donkey riding,
undeniably homeless young fellow pulls out some state of the
art, globally linked, satellite phone - can you believe that shit,
a satellite phone, this kid has the look of a save the children
poster boy, dressed in the height of panhandler fashion, riding
a protruding ribbed donkey, he most probably slept on car
hoods at night, as did the dogs, yet, he still manages to buy a
satellite phone and pay the monthly bills, my jaw came down
to about my chest while I was thinking: I don't have enough
credit for a goddamn cable contract, shit, and here's this
starving little bastard with a satellite phone and a donkey, it
was right then and there that I decided to really beat hell out
of that kid, take his donkey, his cell phone, knock him on his
ass and say something like welcome to New York fucker, and
as I walked towards him, a pack of stray dogs came from an
alley that I hadn't noticed, there was 7 or 8 of them, looking
diseased and frenzied, and I got nervous, turned that walk
into a run, grabbed the kid by one of his rags, tossed him onto
the street, satellite phone skidding across the cracked
pavement, rabid dogs closing in for the kill, and I just rode

that starving donkey to freedom.

Now that's a story about everything! Fucken piñatas and fighting horses, that's not literature!)

and now I'll turn it over to John:

I slide into the seat to take a look at what the Arab has written, I go through it once, open another beer, twice, then turn to him and say:

this is shit man, pure shit, no one cares about homeless kids with cell phones and donkeys, these guys want SEX and ACTION, not one long sentence about a late night in Cairo.

well I think it's a good story, much better than what you're putting out.

ah fuck that, I'm putting out top notch shit here.

yeah, yeah, well, I don't think so, anyway, I gotta get going, you want another beer before I leave?

sure, thanks man, talk to you later on.

and the Arab walks out, I sit and think about an electro-magnetic masturbation suit, now that would be a fine thing to have, I'd wear it constantly, I'd blast those stimulus rays at my balls and ass till I ran out of come, till I short circuited the thing from overuse, ah shit, me and my pipe dreams, enough already, time to get back to the writing, I pull up a fresh page and start typing:

Late Night in Cairo

Once I was walking around Cairo, it was about one in the morning, and in Egypt, when the sun goes down . . .

⊗ AT LEAST I'M HONEST

I just can't respect all these guys -

I'm too busy

with the mirror
and dancing in hallways
making myself laugh
and playing in the dirt - I dig a hole, six feet deep,
and I bury what they write,
and even the worms
choose to stay away.

⊗ ANY KIND OF ESCAPE

any kind of escape - I'll take it:

books, music, good movies, the right woman, one of my
favorite women
airmailing me tabs of demerol (4 baby whites?) 24hr drinking
spells that cut off my ties with this odd, odd reality, cocaine
vision-crawling into the sewer-cowered in a cave, just
any
kind of escape -

(playing guitar, I'm inhaling smoke, I'm typing my
rough poems, I'm
fucking disconnected - don't you get it(?) I
no longer need the newspapers(!) there's only
one headline
that holds any meaning for me: 'Go Nowhere!')

any kind of escape -

paintings, sketches, long legs stepping from a New York
Yellow, drowning
inside another so like the white paper when it darkens-pen
moves-orchestra builds-some

grand finale-crescendo-ink, like a jotted pregnancy-all these
drunken thoughts-my insightful nights - oh
honey, all I need
is any kind of escape-any kind, go ahead, throw it on the table
and
I'll take it.

And who said the depression was over?

Kamikaze pilot grin as I run out the door -

Hangman knot
tied snug from Burberrys
as I jump down the stairs -

100 mile an hour DWI with closed eyes on the A-train -

Electric chair enthusiasm
shuffling my feet
up West 3rd -

Overdose hungry standing in front of big buildings -

Swan dive bliss
paints my face
in an elevator -

There's no 'Good Morning, how's it going?' cause it's tough
trying to talk
around all this lead (.45 caliber mouth piece helps keep the
mind blank - and why do I need the mind blank? So that I can
sell my body
to the company morgue
without dreaming
of a vacation in Maryland,

maybe

painting a bulls eye
across my back.)

and maybe

u just can't take it any more
there's pressure from every angle and the streets
are looking better

everyday

and maybe u just weren't built for this
(I sure as shit know that I wasn't - I was built to drink beer
and shoot guns and spend mad nights with my lunatic blonde
smoking green dope and getting filthy
stinking

dirty

sweaty

oh . . . yeah, honey)

and maybe
there ARE a million different escape routes
but
there's only ONE
definite
way out (hangman's noose - loops of invitation and bury me
in the deep dark ground without a care in the world hi-ho)

and maybe
u can forget novelty
and possession (what a man really needs
is freedom)

and maybe
u can forget friends
and family (what a man really needs
is freedom)

and maybe

u've got the same

fucking, mind-body-soul killing (demons) digging 40 hour
talons into the small of ur back and what they're really tryin
to get at is ur back bone cause once that's gone it's all
jellyfish lifestyle and spineless thought pattern and welcome
to the real world fucker, leave ur pointless little heart in a box
by the door and that's a swell looking tie ur wearin today,
drinks with the missus after 18 holes and didn't my daughter
look oh so pretty in the winter land concert at her school this
year? (sorry,

shit

all I wanted to write was demons,
just that one word - demons - I was gonna ask
if you had the same ones
as myself
but
if u've gotten this far, well . . . .

**A man walks into a psychiatrists offices and says "doc, I
have a problem, I think I'm god"**

"There's crow's beaks"

and they dart in at my chest,
ripped skin on the sidewalk - fingers across the keyboard
- I'm typing thunderbolts and so I
really don't mind, it's

all

right . . .

"There's tiger's claws"

and they rake fire through my stomach,
runny guts in the jungle - fingers across the keyboard - I'm
typing earthquakes so it really doesn't bother me, it's

o.

k . . .

"There's snake's fangs"

and they slide simple into the flesh, paralyzed mind, my head
in the clouds - I'm
typing tsunami waves and
I'm typing volcanoes,
flash floods and hurricanes, I'm typing my own
'big bang'

BIG BANG

(see what I mean, and if I were to yell 'Let there be light'
I think it would happen:

a pitch black television screen, a wall of complete darkness,
nothing,
totally empty
until ("Let there be LIGHT!")
specks of dust,
twist, dancing through empty space,
and gasses
meet, swirling and merging with rocks and
the Sun
would just BLINK on, super large and bright yellow -
rays across the cosmos) and it would all be the work of

my fingers -

worn down to the bone, stubs on the keyboard, blood across
the page - I'm
typing . . .

a man of vision

(important part of the conversation)

(Me) How about NO - the answer is no, I can't help you
move out of your apartment - much more important things
than you to take care of today.

(She) John, you keep talking to me like that and you can
forget any chance you might have had for some ass.

Already have.

So, you're saying that you've given up all hope, huh?

Ah, shit, ass isn't something you HOPE for. I can BUY ass if
I wanted to - I can go to the local meat market and PICK UP
ass - you don't HOPE for ass - you hope that you'll
eventually find someone that loves YOU for YOU - not if
you were a little more like this or a little less like that, just
YOU - now that's something to hope for.

(And did I say any of this?
Of course I did - the heart pumps and it's a LOUD,
vicious,
fast
pump that shakes my ears and I get floaters in my eyes, those

squiggly little spots you sometimes get after you yawn, or
sneeze, but
you can't tell any of this from my voice. My voice is steel.
My voice is boulders. Strong, immovable, resolute - you can't
tell that I'm scared of what I'm saying and, as always, I know
I'm only hurting myself,
and her,
but the only thing I can do
is be a dick. It's my escape hatch - my contingency plan-
'When all else fails, be a dick! And if that doesn't work, then
be an even bigger dick! Act real smug and indifferent and
laugh in her face kinda thing while sucking on a beer (that's
what I'm doing now-Live Coverage! The Dempsey Network-
bringing you the latest and most up to date news about some
jack off kid,
yelling in a dark room). When all else fails,
be a dick!')

(She) So what are you saying? You don't love me anymore?

(Me) Baby, I love you lots. I love you like I love
hemorrhoids, like I love syphilis, shit, I love you like I love a
positive HIV test.

Fuck you John.

Fuck you honey.

(Phone click - conversation terminated - and (who's that little
lamb in the corner) maybe I shouldn't've said all that (wiping
at his eyes)? I light a cigarette, knock off the beer, and type
this up: The Dempsey Network, yeah, sure, big lights, I'm not
hurt, sure, she means nothing, not a thing, when all else fails,
I'm fine, everything's perfect, be a dick, yeah, that's the only
way to handle these situations, The Dempsey Network,
Hollywood, be a dick, sure,
I can see it all now.)

**9 to 5 psychotic-doctor w/ a fetish-drunk at the wheel w/ a
joint in my mouth: 'Daydreams can turn on a man, show
sharp teeth and snarl.'**

pipe dream driven

and deewee bound (Excuse me, Sir?

Yes?)
the company morgue - that's what's been keeping me up
lately: 3-4-5 o'clock in the morning, thinking (We've got a
situation, it's 4B, acting up again.

Again?)
something about selling my body
to the company morgue (Yeah, and we've upped the dosage,
enough thorazine to knock out a horse.

A horse, huh?)
because that's exactly what it feels like,
dragging ass to the train (Yes, many cc's, restraints, too.

Horses, hmmm, you know, I've always been rather fond of
horses.)
and through the streets, upstairs
and down hallways, automatic doors and (Huh?

I said that I've always been fond of horses, you know?

No.)
dead-eyed stares, unconsciousness flesh,
paycheck
propulsion system and there isn't a man alive (Oh,
well, you ever see a horse, you know, with the back end,
sticking out of the barn, and sometimes when the sun, it
comes down just right
and lands on the tail the way it does . . .

Sir?)
can avoid the million dollar temptation, it's
one hell of planet and I just (. . . makes it look like silk, you
know, looks soft, like something you'd want to sleep in, build
a bed out of and it's the feeling of being thirsty, being thirsty
and there's . . .

4B, remember Sir?)
crash landed just yesterday, surrounded by
some kinda life form, dull, frozen thoughts and (. . . a whole
jug of lemonade, just sitting there, sweating and the ice cubes
floating and you can see the lemon seeds and just being

thirsty . . .

We've gotta do something Sir!)
rooted in their dull,
frozen lives without a single dream (. . . and all that thirst it
does something to a man, something deep and there's no
denying it, you just, you just gotta drink

Sir?

Goddamnit! What?)
but maybe
you're accustomed to the dull lights,
maybe (4B, he's really cracking up in there, keeps screaming
about The Machine, The Escape Dream.

Hmmm.)
maybe you've got these
real sensitive eyes, pupils
that don't wanna contract (Yeah.

O.k.,
fuck it, put him on a drip! Executive decisions here!
Lead weights round the ankles! Horses . . .) me,
I'm gonna pretend I'm in Mexico
pipe
dream
driven (Thorazine, yes! Horses! (deadly blue steel and outlaw
thoughts)

Yes Sir! (chemical
lobotomy
careless) Now damnit! (and its just so) NOW (so pretty
outside) Damnit! (so nice, so right out there) Hurry! (so nice,
when everything fits) I want that bastard (so right out there)
knocked out!)

Friday Morning email to the blonde

Hey baby - ok - I'm ready to call it quits - seriously - I've
been here all of 15 minutes and I've already had more than
enough - I'm on the edge of doing something either very
crazy or very stupid - I felt better when I was home - sick -
sweating - puking, limping around on my gimp foot - than I

do being here - all is shit on shingles and not an inch of
breathing room - these people are all invalids - they're all
mentally retarded, completely fucked up and stupid as sin -
honestly - if it were up to me I'd build one big machine that
had a conveyor belt which fed everybody into big steel jaws
that would clamp down and crush these rotten fuckers right
outa existence - I'm coughing up brown phlegm and still
I feel like smoking 8 packs of butts and putting down 3
bottles of dewars - thank god it's payday cause I can actually
make it happen - Right? Right! Whoever said that working is
good for you and builds character must've been the most
brain dead, creatively deficient, jackass in the world - I'd kick
that bastard's teeth right down his throat if he was in front of
me - ok sweets - sorry to vent on you like this, but if I don't
then I'll wind up tossing people out of windows - you
wouldn't wanna visit me in jail, would you? -john

**Good time - Nothing - The emptiness - A long poem that
should never have been started**

-.. --- / -. --- - / .-. . .- -.. / - .... / .-- --- .-. -.. ... /

.. ..-. / -.-- --- ..- / .-- .. .. / - --- / .-. . -- .- .. -. / .--

.... --- .-.. .

Everything is empty.
Nothing
stands for anything - NOTHING!

Every
thing
doesn't count for
any
thing.

Every
thing
is empty - every thing is a husk, a carcass, a shell, regardless
of what it is - empty.
Life is empty.
Time is empty.

Time is something that we can only catch a glimpse of; only a fraction of every second belongs to us. My fraction of this second is on this page; this fraction of a second is all that matters - get the picture? No? Well, there isn't enough time to type elaborate explanations; I've got only a few fractions of a few seconds to my name so screw it, insert an excerpt from Tom Wolfe, the one from Electric Kool-Aid Acid Test, the one which describes the lag in perception inherent within humans, yeah, that's the one - back to it . . . yesterday stands for nothing and tomorrow is an abstract concept, even the entirety of today is empty - this second is all that matters, this breath, this thought,

toss everything else from the window: memories out the window, hope out the window, throw your heart from the window and allow it to stain the sidewalk, throw mother from the window and listen for her wail, smile wide, laugh at father with the hand-axe, connect one end of a hose to the tailpipe, start the engine,

crack the bedroom window,

and sweet dreams to all...lately

I've found myself

in a very

serene

state of mind, calm thoughts and rational actions, I've come to a great

and deep,

profound understanding, yeah,

that's it - I've come to understand futility, I've come to understand importance: All of our actions are an exercise in futility, nothing

that is ever accomplished will hold even a trace of importance; there is nothing unequal on this god blasted terrain, we are all

equally

unimportant - one death is as good as the next and your death is only a baby step, only a link in a chain, get used to this, you are only a tiny dot on the map - only a tiny dot - nothing that you will ever do is of any consequence - barricade the

school doors, set fire to the building, children will sip boxed
juice and wonder why it's become so warm - perfect, get 'em
while they're young and there will be less to clean up in the
future...we need to prepare for these things. Take me for
instance. I've adopted a strict regimen of coffee, aspirin,
hydro-codeine and domestic beer, 2 daily masturbation
sessions - a fucking champion is what I am, ready, primed,
all set
to swallow the flame,
to swan dive from the earth,
to shake hands with the coffin maker and laugh out loud in
the dark . . . but,
I shouldn't start this thread; you see,
I've got volatile DNA, carry my history like a monkey -
John, I've never heard you mention your grandfather, what
ever happened to him?
a suicide case.
and his grandfather?
another suicide case.
and the grandfather before him?
the same.
so it skips a generation?
tick-tock
excuse me?
I said tick-tock, you know, like clockwork.
oh, so then what do you think is gonna happen to you?
well, I do have a brother, gives me a 50 percent chance.
brother's keeper?
always . . . like I said, shouldn't go down this road, makes me
think too much, causes disturbances, black thoughts,
not what I need,
I need blue thoughts, yellow thoughts, or better yet,
blank thoughts, I need an emptiness . . . I get out onto the
street. Blobs bounce up and down - dangerous. The blobs
suck up all energy in sight - leave empty matter in their wake
. . . I get in an automobile. Drive to a bar. Buy my ticket to
emptiness . . . wake up at my parent's house -
grab an old towel and wipe blood off the fender of my auto
. . . I will not answer my phone for the next few days, all

communication should come in electronic format,
new addressing information to follow, maybe somewhere in
Europe, yeah, now that would be the ideal . . . chew 500
milligrams of xanax, burn the rag and fall asleep . . . wake up
for an appointment with the dentist -
are you sure you want to be put under anesthesia for this?
yes.
it's really a very simple procedure.
doesn't matter.
and you understand the risks of going under?
yes . . . 2000 milligrams to darkness . . . I can chew my own
death as if it were bubble gum,
but the dentist is another story completely . . . wake up
missing teeth. I feel buzzed -
is someone here to drive you home?
yeah, waiting outside.
o.k. here's a prescription for the pain, no solid food or
smoking for two days . . . I get outside, put a cigarette into the
numb hole in my face, get behind the wheel and swerve home
. . . home-home - at home in my parent's house,
a 25 yr old screw up with a spotty track record, just another
fuck up, just another blob bouncing up and down to some half
hearted beat (da-doomb) . . . reach for the flask on my desk, a
birthday present - healthy amount down the throat, shut off
the lights, good times, sure, they just keep on coming . . .
¿Juan?
¿Juan? ¿qué no tiene razón?
nada.
no, es de alguna importancia, me puede decir.
es justo ese, joda, no sé, es justo ese este mundo entero es la
mierda, no hay nada aquí para cualquier de nosotros,
precisamente un derrote después de otro después de otro, aún
es los sueños son sin valor.
es decir mucho para considerar.
sí ello is - una situación muy deprimente.
en realidad - yeah, en realidid -
it's like fighting an undeniable undertow, like being sucked
out to sea . . . become surrounded by your own death and you
begin to make realizations, you realize that all you've ever

fought for is pointless, that all you've ever loved is empty,
that all your moments have been wasted . . . chemical
imbalance? This girl named Dianne gave me a hit of x and 40
minutes later I noticed the change. My heart sped up, faster
and faster and soon it was too fast and I was sweating,
shaking,
too much speed and Dianne noticed the shape I was in. I was
a rectangular with sharp edges and I kept trying to roll into a
circle - it was an
internal
conflict - and so she handed me two tabs of vicodin and I
started to relax.
My edges smoothed out and I became a circle. I rolled out of
her apartment. I rolled down the street. I rolled past cars and
dogs and trains and yuppies. I rolled past killers and priests
and locksmiths
and pornographers. I rolled out past the city limits and onto
the highway . . . came to the mountains - rolled up the side of
the tallest one I could find.
I reached the top . . . and there was a wolf waiting for me.
The wolf took me out of my circle. Shaped me into a man and
this made me upset. I was happier as a circle. I wanted to
remain as a circle and this goddamned wolf came along and
ruined my shape, opened it's jaws -
have you ever slept with a wolf?
no, but I don't care about any of that, turn me back into a
circle.
have you ever felt the wolf's teeth, bearing down on your
neck?
no, turn me back into a circle.
only if you sleep with me . . . I slept with the wolf.
It took 4 hours.
Afterwards, the wolf turned into a woman and the woman
offered me a cigarette. I took it - noticed that it was lit when
she handed it to me - not sure how she did that.
I smoked on the mountaintop, finished my cigarette and
pitched it away. I was feeling tired . . . in the hospital there
was gauze on my chest and they gave me medicine. I was not
in pain but I accepted the medicine . . . it carried me far

away . . . for long periods . . . months maybe . . .
do you remember what happened to you?
what happened to *me*?
yes, *you*, we're trying to figure it out.
have I turned back into a circle yet?
a circle?
yes a circle, the wolf said . . .
the wolf?
yes, she said that if I slept with her she'd turn me back into a
circle.
why a circle?
so that I can roll away - why else?
over to the psyche ward . . . they put me in another part of the
hospital and it was filled with maniacs. I took a lot of
medicine but I never seemed to get any better, just further and
further away and I still had the gauze on my chest and so one
day I pulled it off and underneath was a tattoo. A large tattoo,
of a wolf and when I saw that I screamed and so they gave
me more medicine, but it wasn't the right medicine because I
continued being a man and what I really wanted was to be a
circle and forget about the wolf and I knew that it wouldn't
happen in a hospital and so one night I went to the nurse'
station and what I did there was make friends . . .

I went every night,
made friends with every nurse,
and soon they figured me as harmless . . . dropped their guard
and once they dropped their guard I picked up a metal stapler
and what I did then was . . . left the hospital, released on my
own reconnaissance, yeah, that's it, no blood involved . . . got
in touch with Dianne - asked her to help me become a circle
again - it took two hits of the x and only one of the vicodin.
An improvement? Yes,
I believe it was, allowed me to roll on out of there,
get to where I needed to go . . . certain places . . . do what I
needed to do . . . certain things - there are certain things
beyond human comprehension, yeah,
big forces - there are big forces out there. They hang out past
the limits of our stubborn and inflexible mentality,
inexplicable things that defy all we've ever known - and I

was guided by these big forces, by these inexplicable things,
and they told to me to head west and so I headed west . . . I
rolled out to San Diego, over the border and made Tijuana . . .
from there I was guided across valleys, up hills and through
water, past shotgun shacks and shoeless muchachos,
past taco stands and toothless senoritas,
past goats, past children, down a stretch of beach and finally
to a hut
built out of driftwood and there was an old man there (long
white hair, long white beard, looked about 150 yrs old, but
strong, all muscle, a rag wrapped round his torso, a brown
leather pouch
was hanging off his waist) and I knew he was waiting for me
. . . big forces . . . pulled me out of my circle . . . stayed calm
because his eyes told me to do so (intent can always be
determined through the eyes, let' you know what's really
inside a man) and I was on my back, and I was on the beach
and the old man piled sea grass beneath my head, pulled a
blackish, stringy tobacco from his pouch (smelled like mint)
and a clay pipe, struck a match, lit the whole thing up,
and passed it over . . . I was coughing - bright sparks shot
across my eyes - my chest itched and I was light headed - I
heard seagulls and looked up - they flew in circles - right
above me - the old man covered me in sea grass - smoke
drifted from my nostrils - mint taste in my mouth - the
seagulls in circles, seemed like they were watching me - more
sea grass and my entire body covered except for the eyes - the
seagulls - and then the old man struck another match, took the
flame to the sea grass - the seagulls - and the sea grass caught
fire, and I was covered in the sea grass, and soon I was
covered by the fire and the seagulls flew closer, the biggest
one: only a foot above me, and the flames didn't hurt and the
old man was smiling as he looked down the length of my
body, down towards my legs, and I saw smoke coming off the
sea grass, coming off my legs, and I saw the big seagull,
swoop down and land by my feet, it opened it's mouth,
cawed, no,
it screamed, sounded like a women being paddled about the
ass,

and then it began to inhale the smoke
coming off my body . . .
It started at my feet. Sucking up the smoke and where my feet
once were I saw an empty space, my feet were in the smoke
and the smoke was in the seagull and I began to realize what
was happening. The smoke was coming off my legs now and
the seagull inhaled it and my legs disappeared, and then my
thighs, and then my torso,
and then my chest was gone
and I was only a head
covered in smoke
and then I was only the smoke
and then I was inside of the seagull . . . 2 months . . . 2
dimensional view through the eyes . . . no hunger . . . for
anything . . . no lust, no fear, no strangled ambition . . . 2
months . . . across water, mountains, through towns, down
streets, moon, sun, clouds, wind
whistles as it's cut by the seagull's wings . . . reflection . . .
time to think . . . about Miller, Hemingway, Cervantes,
Bukowski, screw it! I'm a drunken Castaneda,
in love with girl from Ipanema . . . reflection . . . never touch
the rhyming poetry . . . reflection . . . unhappy with the globe?
Then lower your expectations - it'll curb the disappointment -
allows you to take the next the step . . . 2 months . . . inside of
the seagull . . . I make the Long Island Sound . . . a familiar
stretch of beach . . . (Scene: 2 young boys sit on wooden
benches by the shore, one carries a blow gun, follows the
flight of my seagull with almond brown eyes, leads the course
by a few inches, inhales, deep, filling his lungs, squints and
. . . phwoot . . .
My seagull falls from the sky . . .
Boy #1: oh, you got him!
Boy #2: I told you I would.
and right in the neck too! look at him squirm!
we should probably finish him off, put him out of his misery.
yeah, it's the right thing to do.
yes, the right thing - should I shoot him again?
no, use a rock, I saw a big one over by the bench.
all the way back there?

yeah.

screw that, I'm not goin all the way back there for a rock,
besides, look at him, he'll be dead in a minute, let's just get
outa here . . . the two hunters mount up, ride away on BMX
bicycles and we end the scene) . . . I watch through the
seagull eyes, feel a tightening sensation, a squeezing-
constriction of the seagull muscles, something pushing me
from behind, from the sides, forcing me up
and out . . . the seagull opens it's beak . . . HACK . . . coughs
me up onto the sand . . . Sandy say's that I can make 5.50 an
hour working the concession stand at the beach. Plus I get
free burgers and soda. I take her up on it.

Working at the beach you meet allot of people. I meet 2:
Carter and the little Spaniard.

Carter - he's a lifeguard, a drunkard, a philosopher, a
womanizer, a chauvinist, a drug addict, a molester of young
children and he invites me to head down to Florida with him
at the end of the summer.

The little Spaniard - she's a bikini, a sex-bomb, a coke freak,
a stepdaughter, a brunette with this magically round ass that
listens to Jane's Addiction while I lick out her insides. She
wants to come to Florida with us.

In October: The three of us head down I-95 in a Chevy
Lumina. I eat a hit of Jesus Christ blotter and melt into the
back seat. We take shifts driving and when it's my turn I slip
behind the wheel ginger snap smiling and my pupils dilated
and all systems go with the little Spaniard saying that Carter
is definitely asleep and do I mind if she puts her head on my
lap . . .

why . . . of course not sweety.

oooh, what's this Johnny?

that's my navigator, he tells me where to go.

well, I think it's too stuffy in there for him - maybe we should
take him out.

yes, I think that's a good idea.

look, he likes it out here, see how happy he is!

the happiest.

but he might get cold.

maybe.

should I try warming him up?
yes, that would probably be best honey.
mmm, glub, glub, mmm, oooh
Johnny . . . Florida is fine in the winter, the rent is cheap, the
cigarettes are cheap, the beer is cheap - DIRT Cheap - and it's
still warm. Warm enough to swim and Carter teaches me to
scuba dive. We take acid and drive to the water. Good times.
We spit into our masks and wipe them down. Check
regulators, valves, air supply, zippers, weight belts, knives,
fins, minds and walk towards the waves. He gives me basic
instructions and I learn quickly - breath is measured, I
memorize all the hand signals, the acid rides my thoughts and
we duck under the water . . . its all very,
peaceful . . . fish come in different shapes and colors and
shapes and colors and Carter points out a school of silvery,
missile shaped fish swimming out in the distance . . .
barracuda . . . signals me to swim down to the bottom and
that's what I do . . . pulls his diving knife, ties a long string to
the handle, sticks it into the sand, and swims over to where I
wait . . . points his index and middle fingers at his face, the
signal to look, and then points to where the knife is . . . I
watch and he starts giving the string these gentle little tugs,
just enough to make the blade dance,
catch the sunlight,
and reflect it back . . . instant reaction, the barracuda dart out
from the depths, lightening fast movement of scales and teeth
and they're attacking the blade, one by one, opening their fat
jaws and trying to bite it in half. Each time they come away
bloody. And the more that Carter works the string the harder
they charge and soon I can see their jaws hanging loose, the
muscles ripped, shattered teeth, heavy blood
and still
they go after the blade . . . something inside of me . . .
becomes unhinged, I make a bad connection and I have to get
out of there, the acid, good times, the barracuda is every man,
the knife is every woman . . . no matter how many times a
man gets hurt, he will always return to that same blade . . .
it's a reflex I'm told, later that night -
Carter: you see, the barracuda is helpless in this situation; it's

their natural instinct to attack anything that flashes like that -
looks like bait fish to them.
Me: it bugged me out, made me think about things.
oh yeah, what kind of things?
all kinds, depressing things, the futility of love.
the futility of love?
yes.
the barracuda made you think of that?
yes . . . and the little Spaniard doesn't like this . . . knows I'm
onto something . . . she quickly cuts four lines on the table
top and passes me a section of the drinking straw we had
chopped up. I'm a Hoover vacuum cleaner with a super
charger - make the four lines disappear and grab her by the
ass, numb-jaw-smiling, and she's happy with these results . . .
the next day we are down to our last three hits of acid. We sit
around on the couch and wait for it to take hold. I read a
paperback copy of
Naked
Lunch.
When the words fall of the side of the page
I know that I'm doing all right.
Put the book down. Carter is in the shower singing Sinatra.
The little Spaniard is staring at the television. It's a
commercial for some movie. Some 15 yr old bastard - got the
fastest pitch ever seen - the little fucker is on the mound
wearing a Cub's jersey. He's winding up. Twisting his lips.
Checking the signals. Then lets it rip . . . phwoosh . . . right at
the screen and that ball comes right through the glass and
bears down on me, I tilt my head at the last second, watch it
sail over my shoulder, flames coming off it and moving
awfully fucken fast . . . cutthroat television . . . there's a red
carpet but now it's lava and I pick my feet up so that I won't
burn.
The little Spaniard doesn't seem to mind, Carter is still
singing Sinatra, I'm scared shitless . . . fold my legs up and
start whining (John, what's wrong with you?) . . . search for a
way out . . . (John?) the window . . . talk to my muscles and
they tell me that they're ready . . . (John, try not to freak out
now baby.) through the window and down the hill to

grandma's house we go . . . (Just try and stay calm.) I giggle
at the thought, remember the barracudas, wave a goodbye to
the Spaniard (What are you doing John?) and jump through
the glass . . . shit,
running off,
joining this special kinda circus:
Trapeze artists with typewriters strapped across their bellies
drop poems on the crowd from a hundred feet up. Bearded
women hand script novels of European travel and sexual
enlightenment with razor blade gusto. Lion tamers whip at
the page! The strong man lifts heavy philosophy! Knife
juggler stabs at the word! And I
see movie rights and butter ass future and my barge fantasy
sailing on stolen oil drums, peeling
dead skin off brown shoulders while waiting on the
BIG BITE and maybe
it's you
that doesn't fit into the picture . . .

big-top dreams,
some hard lines -

You've got exactly
what it needs to make it. Shit! These fuckers may not know,
but you were built for this.
Predestined
and guided
by BIG FORCES. (background plays a band by the name of
Neutral
Milk
Honey,
the words are: 'cause there are some lives you live and some
you leave behind')
Hey Johnny, how many times have you walked away from
death, just so you can sit here, right now, and type all these
lines?
Remember your first car? Remember flipping it 4 times, roof
caving, 4 lanes, oncoming traffic, kicking out the back
window and smiling, as if the laws of physics, and the human
anatomy

have no bearing
on your personal,
physiological
state? Remember jumping off that train? Or how about when
you were twelve and lost in Cairo and that degenerate fuck
grabbed you and your 9-year-old brother, covered mouths
while dragging the both of you
to a hole in some foreign wall and that flash of a curved
blade,
and you were just fast enough
to snatch it out of his hands while he was listening for
footsteps
and you didn't even think, just a quick slash
and his surprised,
dying
eyes and then all that red while you grabbed your brother's
hand and yelled 'Run,
Fucking Run!' And there's more - how many times have you
jumped out of planes?
(5 times, all at 13 thousand feet) How much coke have you
snorted? (enough to kill a stable) And do you think pills
extend the life cycle? (pop-pop of hydro-codeine, teeth
crunch, beer chaser, while slapping the left cheek)
Hey John,
think the boss will say anything about all that purple on your
face? Oh, and by the way,
your teeth
are looking real good,
plus that nipple like growth,
jutting off the right elbow, a fucken lady magnet, cultivate the
bastard! Feed him radiation and douse him with pheromones!
Rub him in the moonlight 'cause he's nothing but a keeper
. . . bull-
shit.
I was scared it would be something cancerous and so when I
got back to New York I made an appointment with the
dermatologist.
He covered the growth with liquid nitrogen and a week later
it turned black. 2 weeks later it fell off and so I started to look

for a job. Problem is, you need to be good at something or
else you just won't fit into the machinery of things.
You need to be good
with something, anything, maybe with a guitar or a baseball
bat,
or with a computer or a paintbrush or a typewriter or with a
hand-whip. Or maybe you just need the right face, yeah,
a t.v. face with the well oiled smile and all the right scripts.
Or how about a camera, some type of photographer, yeah,
adjusting shutter speed and loading kodachrome,
kodachrome, kodachrome . . . but,
I'm no good at any of these things.
I'm just a pretender - a liar, a fake.
I've got good camouflage,
but I'll only be able keep my secret for so long. And then
once I'm discovered
I'll be out on my ass.
It'll be understood that I don't belong.
That I don't fit into the machinery.
It'll be understood that I'm empty, that I'm just like
everything else - a husk, a shell, a blob, a wolf, a priest, a
pornographer, a mother, a locksmith . . . just like everything
else . . . I'll be empty . . .

Half-something and not enough of the other

I must be half-mad to walk around like this
ripped, burned, swollen,
perpetually
on the verge of something,
yet never quite sure
what that something is.

And I must be a half-wit to keep pushing like this
stumbling, bloody, broken and
knowing
that it's right around the corner
yet never really knowing
what
it is.

And I must be half-dead to keep living like this
gambling, typing, every day
a suicide and
feeling
as if I'm almost there,
so close, I'm closing in -

but closing in on what?
Headed where?
Not sure . . .
but I know all about the others,
and there's no
guessing games
with those guys

just

words.

❦ LADIES & GENTLEMEN - WE'VE GOT A FIGHTER

Surrounded
by silver bugs I rode a black scorpion - the tail poised
with venom at the ready - pirate grin splits
my round moon face and every breath
an uphill battle.

Surrounded
by black scorpions I rode a wild striped snake - the fangs
exposed
with venom at the ready - senile smile
plastered across my round moon face and every step
an uphill battle.

Surrounded
by wild striped snakes I rode a tie-dyed komodo - the claws
outstretched
with venom at the ready - outlaw smirk

stapled to my round moon face and every word . . .
Surrounded

by breath I took a step backwards
and all my words
rolled down a hill and I followed smiling, typing about
dragons
and snakes, scorpions
and silver bugs and I realized
that every ending
is just the beginning
of yet another
uphill battle.

ॐ SCREW THIS

Screw this-
I should be writing beer commercials, or maybe sitcoms
instead of this: 3 a.m.
on a Sunday morning - in love with eight women and I'm in
bed alone,
working at these lines, I'm drinking Michelob and
laughing
too loud, (and

maybe I really am sick?)
laughing at it all, (yeah, I'm sick alright, sick of . . .) all of it,
it's just

too funny, (sickening)

gambling away life in order to lay down a few words - too
funny, too
fucken funny (and what's so funny john? everything,
everything is too funny, it's all just

goddamned hilarious(!),

and I'm laughing cause I know all about it, yeah that's it, I
know

all about it. hmmm,
and what exactly,
do you know all about? well,
I know that . . .) I won't get past 30 like this, I can't,
NO WAY,
someTHING is bound to suck me into the void, someTHING
is waiting right around the corner, whether it be
tombstone curiosity,
or some
half drunk cab driver, asleep at the wheel,
or maybe even the bottle
or the pills or the powders
or the smoke or the random sex scene with some alien
female,
heavy red lips, body pressed to the bricks, moaning in an
alley, midtown Manhattan:

20 dollars of love hangs wet around my waist and oooh I'm
just so

damned

smart

and

beautiful -

Aren't I?

(yes john, pure beauty, pure brilliance, that's you, don't let
anyone
tell you different. oh,
sweets,
don't you worry bout that, I won't, besides,
I'm 99 percent deaf
when it comes to listening to other people, well, except for
you of course, I always
listen to you - and you know why?
no, tell me - tell me!
because you always say the right things to me, you always
know how to make me smile.
oh,

do I really john? you know, I really try to make you happy.
I know you do, and it always works. that's why you're my
special pet, my

one and only.

oh,
do you really mean it?
of course I do,
with every bloody little fiber
pumping rancid and ridiculous
in my rotten little heart,
with every dead little brain cell
floating aimless through my head - I mean it all honey.
oh john, I don't think your heart's all that rotten.
well, no matter, all that matters is that it's us two against the
world, just us sweets!
just us? are you sure? you're not just saying that,
are you?
no,
not at all sugar, no way - I'm all
hurt feelings, depression and teardrops when you're not
around. oh
john.) (and maybe
I really am sick - interior love affair with an
alter ego - screams of bipolarity - mentally defect and
sociologically inept - hanging by a
t
h
r
e
a
d
and all that
fine feeling
of being outa touch - Disconnection - phone's off the hook
and the door's
dead bolted, drawn curtains
in a dark room, a mouthful of dirt and a head full of poetry, a
gut full of beer and this is only the beginning - I'm still going

over here - pumping and
burning - all hands on deck - body like a lightening rod -
supercharged - cigarette in my mouth - cocaine frenzy -
driving towards the edge - I'm screaming: No Stop Signs! No
Red Lights! Keep moving!
Faster!
And if you realize
that your brakes are bad, well
then jam on the gas! Move Faster! Faster! Speed
Damnit!) And do you see what I mean? No way I'll make 30-
some drastic
uh,
lifestyle changes would have to be made and
baby, I'm one stubborn fuck - set in my ways and happy in a
rut, I

like the underbelly of existence,
I like the street side perspective,

SHIT!

I like the scars that crisscross my forehead and make me look
like some post-op lobotomy and I like my
brown eyes red and my
intoxicated
thought process that allows me to type real freely, and put
down whatever the hell I want without a care - not a care, not
a care about any thing/body else and
who ELSE is out there? Typing sad songs, on a Sunday
Morning,
5 a.m. with shaky hands - in love with eight women and in
bed alone,
working at lines, drinking Michelob, and laughing
too loud (and maybe
you're sick as well?) (no, I'm most definitely not sick john -
you, on the other hand, you've got some issues, some
problems to work out, you need a couch and a psychoanalyst
and maybe a few days
in a nice
quiet
white room

with sweet nurses and mood altering medication - know what
I mean?) Yeah
I think I do: crocodile tears scuttle down a mannequin's
cheeks, a plastic arm outstretches . . .

and it's a joy buzzer handshake - high voltage cattle prod pats
on the back -

Care for a swim? (electric eels in the pool, but I assure you,
completely harmless) -

Bite to eat? (live wire tossed salad
dashed
with a magnesium
diboride dressing, and it's super, simply super, the chef's
specialty!) -

Mind grabbing your ankles? (aquatic electrode enema, will
literarily shock shit out of your system and leave you as fresh
and as faceless as some pretty lil microchip comin off the
assembly line) -

Welcome home Mr. Dempsey!

shock -

more shock -

eventual reconditioning -

"Mind grabbing your ankles?"

Why,

of course not,
be my personal
and humble type pleasure sir . . .) Aghhh!...(maybe
I really am sick?) 7 a.m.
on a Sunday morning - in love with eight women and I'm in
bed alone,
working at these lines, I'm drinking Michelob and
laughing
laughing
way
too

loud.

Nothing quite like it

The beauty of it
lies in not giving a fuck
in not caring
in saying
screw the audience
and screw the reader
and to hell with the critic
and lets piss on the reviewer
and toss acceptance from the window,
because who really needs that anyway?
And while we're at it, what the hell is acceptance? (haven't
got a clue, screw it!) I
like to hold rejection to my chest
I like to cuddle with it
I like to talk softly to it, I say,
hello baby rejection, how are you doing today, have you
missed me, I know, it's only been a few days, but I miss you
already, and rejection talks back to me, says sorry,
but upon further consideration, doesn't fit in with the rest of
our features, we do not print this sort of material, the content
is
nothing short of tasteless, and then I hold rejection even
closer, squeeze tighter, sigh, oh, yes, my
sweet,
sweet
rejection - there's
nothing
quite like it.

ℂℛ ROB CORPSES?

doesn't get any better, does it?

the same old words
produced by the same old key strokes
the musty thoughts, grown moldy in closets,
the stale sentiments, lying arranged on shelves,

- dust covered lines -

all of our poems
have been packaged: boxed and read and then re-read and re-
worded and re-worked and it's the 21'st century and it seems
as if
originality
is a thing of the past . . .

"We have attained cookie cutter production rates!
Get your Love poems in aisle 7.
Teen angst in 6,
Horror in 5 along with Gay/Lesbian in 4,
Erotica in 3,
Self-Help in 2,
Death
in 1 . . . "

Death
in
1 . . . Ha,

all you

poets

out there, you just keep on typing,
stock those shelves.

❧ ONE HELL OF A DIRTY JOKE

laid up
in this
rank,
sticky,
stinking
bed - bronchitis and a broken foot - I (could've sworn that I
was indestructible, I)

can't really
breathe or
walk all that well - no appetite,
high fever,
brown phlegm, I'm swallowing pills

and

the woman
has fallen down her stairs
in a fit of wine and there's puss - squirts sweetly from her
bright
shining
pink eyes and

with a rusted table saw,
the giant,
has sliced down to the bone,
his right index finger and the blood
runs oh
so pretty on the rotating metal . . . blade like a painting and

we're all in emergency rooms - broken, drunken and smiling -
doctor's offices - broken-
pharmacy counters - drunken-
in our beds - smiling - mid 20's - young

little kittens
purring
for golden milk with backs arched and
eyes slit and as the big jaws

clamp down
with a lethal
determination: 'Oh
nurse, doctor, mother and baby, our bodies
just weren't designed
to meet our mind's expectations.'

☙ NEW YORK'S FINEST

I hadn't seen the Giant in a while and when I jumped through
his door wearing an eye patch and a red bandana I got
laughter from Brian the Douche, Matty Meat Hands, Mike the
Arab, Tanya the Guinea (she looks like the chick from the
Matrix, maybe a little cuter) Sasha the Shark and Coco the
Mutt.

And I was amped up on speed - crushed/snorted diet pills and
No-Doze - and everybody was doubled over while I walked
around with this
real authentic
pirate drawl, spilling sea terms outa my mouth and 'Dar she
blows!' They were on this
imported,
green beer and I pulled up a stool and someone handed me a
bottle and the night was finally started because now the party
was here,
the good time kid was here,
Johnny
reckless with an eye patch and I gave Sasha the Shark a pinch
on the ass and she turned all red, smiled
oooh
and so I did it a second time because I felt that it was the right
thing to be doing.

Then a joint was passed around and our eyes turned
a burst
blood vessel red
and someone,

I think it might've been
Brian the Douche,
started telling a joke - a woman, a lama and a Chinese guy in
a monkey suit are in a life raft - when 2 cops, foaming at the
mouth with police specials drawn and warrants and badges,
nightsticks so shiny, kicked in the door and ran in the place
like some kinda movie or
cop drama
tv show and all of us (the Douche, Meat Hands, the Arab, the
Guinea Matrix chic, Sasha the Shark and Coco the Mutt (plus
myself!)) sat half-stoned,
and I was the lucky duckling - burning roach pressed to my
lips and I wasn't even thinking,
I just
kept inhaling and inhaling and it was like - bottomless lungs-
and I inhaled some more, my chest
puffing out marvelous and the two cops staring at me and it
felt like everyone was staring at me and no one was saying
anything and - bottomless lungs - inhaling and this thin crack
starts splitting my face - San Andreas Fault - eye patch hangs
crooked - red bandana - and I
completely
lose it, all the smoke in my chest - too much to hold and
green grass grin
loud laughing/coughing/choking/hiccups fly outa my mouth
and my whole body bucking/shaking/spazzing out/beep-
bopping and twitching on the stool, eye patch crooked
and I work it back over my eye and that was the final straw
cause soon as I looked up
those two cops were all hysterical laughter and everybody
else (Brian the Douche, Meat Hands, Mike the Arab, the
Guinea Matrix chic, Sasha the Shark and even Coco the Mutt)
was laughing right along with them and it was one hell of a
scene to be sitting there and smoking dope while two officers
cracked up at you like that and so I asked if they wanted a
beer.

Those two cops sat and drank with us until 4 that morning-
(the warrant was for the guy that lived there right before the
Giant moved in, maybe 3 months ago - I think cops are smart)

- and then they said that their shift was over - time to get back to headquarters, and won't you guys get any shit for drinking on the job - nah, not at all, the chief has got the biggest liver in this city, he's an around the clock drunk. As long as we get our shit done and no one gets hurt, then everything's cool - sounds like a pretty nice gig you guy's got over there - yeah man, only the best for us, shit, we're New York's finest!

ℜ WORDS TO ESCAPE

A way to live.
A shift in perception.
2 percasets
on a Thursday morning.
Words to escape.
A shift in mentality.
I think in 3 languages
on a Thursday morning.
Disruptive thought process.
Irregular heartbeat.
This place is a madhouse
on a Thursday morning. Fed up with the globe?
Grown tired of the air? Commit yourself
on a Thursday morning. Words to escape.
But where you gonna go? I'm gonna type my way out
on a Thursday morning.

ℜ SELF DEFENSE

jazz tune players
four baby blondes
and the young gangster types, they wear velour jogging suits,
gold medallions and clean sneakers
and a jamaican preacher, bongo drums, dreadlocks, the word
of

some lord
a dollar fifty
to hang by a strap
"I'm all covered up in metal, laying in the belly of some
horrible old beast"
fast moving mothers
worker bee's buzzing: stock options bzzzt integrated
risk
analysis goes buzz, I like riding up in the front car, face
pressed to the glass so that I can watch the tracks. They twist
and curve, disappear under my feet and sometimes I imagine
that I'm eating up all that track, that I'm not even on the train
anymore, but that I'm the train itself, chugging and sparking
along and swallowing up all that track and moving so fast that
nothing can catch me, nothing, like I'm some pure form of
perpetual energy and everything else is just small time stuff,
everything else is just steam engine stuff, cotton wheel and
horse drawn wagon type stuff and they can barely see me
because I'm moving so fast and it's a feeling of power, all
that speed and eating all that track and the way the sparks
shoot out from underneath me and all the frozen organisms
just standing stock still while I blast across the landscape
tooting and shrieking, steel wheels grinding, blue sparks
flying and I need all that power, I store it up inside me like a
battery and when the wheels stop turning and the doors slide
open and I flash all that stored up energy at the jazz tune
players
and the four baby blondes
and the young gangster types, in their velour jogging suits,
and the jamaican preacher, with bongo drums and dreadlocks
and the word of
some lord
and they all just
sorta vaporize, fade out, lose consistency and pretty soon
they're all just
no longer there and
that's a good thing, a very
good thing. That West 3rd station

can kill a man in a hundred different ways.

∝ STUMBLING IDOLS

I was in the bathtub,
I was drinking white wine,
I was scribbling my bad poems,
when Hemingway dripped in through the shower faucet.

"Soft,
you're a soft-boiled egg
Dempsey,
and not only that, but you write like woman."

"Thank you Ernie." (I got out of the tub,
dried off,
and got on the toilet)

I was on the toilet,
I was drinking domestic beer,
I was scribbling even worse poems,
when Burroughs reached up through the water.

"You smell like shit Dempsey,
pure
shit,
and that same smell
comes out in everything you type."

"You're a real sweetheart Billy."
(I wiped clean, put on shorts,
and sat on the couch)

I was on the couch,
I was on dewars and coke,
I was scribbling some of the most horrible poems,
when Buke climbed in through the window.

"Your nothing but a fake Dempsey, a phony,
in over your head
and way outa your league."

"Oh Hank, you always know just the right things to say.
(I finished my drink, lit a butt,

and got into bed)

I was lying in bed,
I had one hand under the covers,
I was thinking up my
terrible
little poems and I was beginning to sweat,
when Dempsey (that's right,
Dempsey!)
crawled out from under the mattress.

"Oh, Johnny Boy."

"Yes?"

"Don't you pay any attention to those guys -
you just keep on typing
your sickly sweet poems and keep on stapling
your guts to the page
and pretty soon you'll find out
that you don't need any heroes - all that you really need
is yourself."

"Oh yeah?"

"Yeah. Meet your own standards and you can tell the rest of
the gang to go screw."

"Is that so."

"100 percent buddy."

"Well,
if that's the case,
then I guess you should go screw."

☙ LAST OF THE ARTISTS

You understand,

that there are a million fuckers out there -

pounding at the keyboard

beating at the language
working the letters
and laying it all down -

and that there are a million killers out there -

stabbing at structure
drowning the words
strangling
all the commercial constraints of editorial guidelines and text
book grammar

and laying it all down -

and that there are a million lovers out there -

undressing their sentences
tongue kissing periods and heavy breath typing
gentle caresses
of every phrase, lipstick smudges
running red down the page and
laying it
all down -

and that there are a million writers out there -

I see them on bookshelves
I pick up a handful of their work
I read a hundred of their pages
and not a one of them
is laying anything down . . .

You understand,

Us fuckers

Us killers

Us lovers -

we're all that's left
of a dying breed - we're
the last of the artists.

❧ THE SHORT POEM

I seem to have lost the short poem
and it's a shame-
those
that can say so much
using so little
always leave
the greatest of impacts.

❧ THE ONLY ONE THAT MATTERS

the only one that matters

said the crowd
when Icarus dropped from the sky
as Lee Harvey took aim
and as Armstrong
stepped onto the moon

the only one that matters

as Marylyn stood over that grate - the wind lifting her skirt -
legs barely crossed, just touching at the knees - big city smile
- the camera's bright flash
or when Hitler
raised his arm in salute, that first
evil heil
or when Jimmy
wrote Moonlight Drive in that
one
defining moment, the only
one that matters
and I've spent a trivial
25 years (so far, so damned
young and yet mad) waiting
on that moment,

on that one moment, the moment when I put down the
indes-
tructible line - the one line that will blast everything else from
the page, the line that will make the book racks look paltry,
dull and ridiculous in comparison. The line that will catapult
me from the sidewalk and allow me to butt heads with the
greats (yeah right,
I'm a second rate boxer who snuck into the ring) and it will
be the only line that matters, that one nuclear line, that one
cosmic line that will breathe long after I'm dust in a box, long
after I'm just a name on some gray stone marker, the one that
will be remembered, the one that will change people - yeah,
sure,
that's what I'm waiting on . . . Monday night beautiful down
to half a bottle of wine,
I snort two bumps of valium and plant dry lips on the blonde
she smiles a glucose summer smile
and drips honey down the back of her neck
my tongue at the ready
I shake the Berlin Wall. I watch the vultures wheeling
in panic-stricken circles
and fall from the sky
in a dive-bombing jumble
of blood and feathers and beak and the sun exits stage left as I
drown
in pools of cool cobalt blue . . . that one line, that one moment
- the only one that matters and it could come at anytime
or
anywhere: 4 a.m. on the train or
1 a.m. in the supermarket,
2 p.m. in a bed
or early morning in a car
midnight in a hospital
or midday at a funeral . . . anytime: the cosmos waits for no
one and the gods smile only once in a lifetime - take
advantage of that smile, make sure you're ready to grab onto
that one
all important
moment (the only one that matters!) and hold it to close your

chest, clutch at it,
as if it were a life preserver,
as if it were your one
and only
true love (hi kitten),
as if it were your first born child and allow it to suckle at your
chest, go a step further: tear open the ribcage and replace the
heart, further: split open the skull and replace the brain,
furthest: make it your entire world and leave everything else
to rot,
LEAVE EVERYTHING ELSE TO ROT,
to rot and ruin and decay and everything else will hold you
back unless you let it sail to the floor, everything else will cut
you off at the knees, will leave you struggling to regain
that
one
moment,
the
only one that matters - Be ready!
Don't get caught in the rain with your pants round your
ankles -
Be ready!
Don't let the moment pass you by while you make eyes with
some walking disease -
Be ready!
Don't
allow the Stock-Fucken-Life to rob you like some two-bit
pickpocket with fast hands and no conscience, just
be
fucking
ready! And I pray
that it won't catch me on the job because that's where I'm at
my weakest, at my brain-deadliest. That's when I'm just a
body, devoid of all life and just waiting for the coffin - the
job will not prepare me
(or you)
for the moment - shit, the job is a killing machine,
the job is a trash compacter
retooled

to shred the soul and a soaring timesheet is 5 times as deadly
as a soaring bar tab
(I've been enlightened a thousand times over sitting at the
corner of a bar, but never once
behind a desk). The timesheet speaks of lost hours and of ball
and chain lifestyle - speaks of paycheck addiction - speaks of
corporate junkies getting their fix at the bank while us
suckers dance for nickels and gold stars. The bar tab,
now that's another story - the bar tab screams of long nights
and flirting eyes, of fights gone bad and a split lip in the
mirror, the bar tab SCREAMS LIFE! Life lived! And life
drunk! That's how I want the moment to hit me. I want it to
come down like some gigantic
A-bomb. I want it to blast me off the bar stool and send me
running for The Machine. Yeah,
I want it to hit me when I can stop time with a twist of my
thoughts and I can watch the words
dance behind my eyes, yes (!) frantic words,
that run across the page
and jump in thru your eyes, ready to sit in your brain like
some space-aged tumor and grow and grow and
grow . . . that one moment - the only one that matters, the one
that makes sense out of all this
(disgusted look on my face) breathing that I've been doing,
the one that will let me get down that one line . . . so right,
leaning into the walls, rubber legs, the muscles won't
respond, being sucked into the plaster, soundless yelling,
mouth filled with those delicious needles,
screaming yellows and such,
salvation under water,
I mix crushed glass with her blue eyes and I wait on that one
moment, the only one
that matters . . . now,
what about yourself?

It was the last day of December - turn of the millennium -
middle of Amsterdam-
and within the confines
of the Hotel Inntel, I sat in the bathtub, drinking warm beer
(dead empties sink to the bottom, lifeless - everything else
floats, means that they're alive, means that they're fair game -
Question: Why dance on graves when it's the live fuckers
that force you to look over your shoulder?) I was preparing
myself, squeezing my balls and

"John what the hell are you doing in there?"
"Squeezing my balls."
"Don't give me that shit, you've been in there for over an
hour."
"Alright, I'll be out in a minute."
"Did you drink all that beer?"
"What beer?"
"The beer I saw you take in there with you, it's 8 in the
morning, too early to deal with your blah blah bitching and
nag nag nagging and where the hell are my cigarettes, shit, I
need a smoke, John, bang bang banging open this door before
I . . . "

getting ready, I dry off, throw on musty, wrinkled clothes,
ashtray cologne
beer breath, the phone rings: Mr. Brady? Yes? (I travel under
different names; this time, I'm Mr. Brady) There's a Mr.
Conrad here to see you. Thank you; tell him I'll be down in a
minute.

Elevator, three flights, facial hair and double vision, rust
stained razors carve gentle figure eights, slice up my thought
process into pretty little circles until I'm face to face
with the great
Italian poet. We look at each other:
Ric? Yeah. John? Yup. Something to drink? Of course my
good man,

of course . . .

A deranged
meeting of the minds . . . bar next door . . . 2 pints, Belgian
beer . . . tastes of old cider, apples gone long rotten,
fermented and yeasty, high octane . . .
you know, I saw a couple of pistolero types in here, tough
looking Mexicans with the low slung holsters . . . cigarette
boxes empty themselves, the rolled tobacco jumps between
lips, glows cancerous and serene . . . we're the only ones out
there, all these other guys are typing bubblegum and unicorns
. . . even some of the greats, weren't all that great, just
misunderstood . . . and you can't take these new guys at face
value, shit, these days every one has a plastic surgeon, fixed
noses and tucked cheek poetry, yeah, liposuctioned lines,
Michael Jackson prose and not a real heart in the crowd . . .
yellow fingers drumming against old, stained table top . . .
mix the Time element with an alcohol based conversation and
you will get one of two things, either an extreme truth, or an
undeniable falsehood . . . last night at the Grey Area, 2 grams,
Stardust . . . blonde hash . . . we must . . . retrieve her . . . the
hotel . . . I should call first . . .

Under the low lights of the hotel lobby sits 3 feet
of smoking
blonde
hair - the legs
crossed and blue fog waves
roll out from her nose, hang by the cheeks, suspended
for one
graceful
second . . . 'Ric, this is the blonde, the great American
girlfriend.
Honey, this is the Ric, the great Italian poet.'

And then we we're in a coffee shop, and it might have been
the heavy hash, in the middle of Amsterdam, sitting with the
blonde
and the great
Italian poet at 10 a.m. with mugs of beer
pressed to our faces

or maybe it was our BIG
literary talk
spinning reckless across the table - cluttered, jumbled, half
drunken
words of immortality - but I was feeling good, strong, as if I
had just eaten an entire chicken and a pound of exotic fruit or
maybe even popped speed, bennies, eye-openers, black
beauties and you might not understand this, but I was the
atom bomb, the hydrogen bomb - I was a nuclear reactor! I
was a goddamned powerhouse! My life force was something
radiant, something radiant, blaring, beaming and dazzling. It
was as if I contained so much energy that it was bleeding
from my pores, leaking from my ears and nostrils and there
was a picture show glowing bloody bright and bloody
breathtakingly beautiful behind my eyes:

Ceiling point of view, looking down on myself,
sitting with the blonde
and the great
Italian poet at 10 a.m. with mugs of beer
pressed to our faces and from this angle I can see a slit
beginning to form at the top of my head and some of that
blaring, radiant life force was leaking out of the slit and it was
a violent, blue light, so strong that I could barely look at it, so
bright that it forced my pupils to contract into the tinniest of
tiny black orbs, and the slit began to spread, turning into a
crack and the crack went from my forehead all the way down
to the bottom of my neck and the light was everywhere,
spilling from the crack and slicing through the bar, blasting
through all the people and out the door, across a thousand
streets and down a thousand alleyways, through all the triple
x sex shops and across a thousand red light window cunts all
covered in black lace with garters and the dime store
perfume, on roller skates and in mini-skirts, sweating and
pumping, reeling
in a thousand red light window dreams, and all my violent,
blaring and radiant life force just cutting right through them
and turning it all, dream and cunt and alleyway and street and
people and bar, all of it, all of Amsterdam, all of it,
to dust.

The picture show ends and I'm back in the bar, sitting with the blonde
and the great
Italian poet with mugs of beer
pressed to our faces and they were talking politics.
Meanwhile
I was having paranoid thoughts,
thoughts of cunts and cracks, violent light and grand scale
destruction. I had to do something before the slit began to
form and so I got up and went to the bathroom. I squeezed
my nuts, splashed my face with cold water, got out, and made
it back to the table. I was feeling along my forehead when the
waitress brought over another round.

Ric: "So John, what do you have planned for the night?"
John: "Not sure yet, I figured on the square, maybe watch the
fireworks, maybe eat some mushrooms.'
"I can see you enjoying that."
"What about yourself?"
 "I'm headed to a party with the wife, a few friends in an
apartment. Actually, I should start heading back to the
station."
 "Alright, let's finish up and we'll walk you over."

We finished up, lit cigarettes, started walking and made the
Centraal Station.

Centraal Station
in the middle of Amsterdam, standing with the blonde
and the great
Italian poet, heavy buzz in the early afternoon, light rain and
disjointed thoughts,
December 31'st, nineteen 99 . . . be careful in the square
tonight John, these Dutchmen are crazy with their fireworks
. . . heel-toe shuffle to a sickly staccato beat . . . learn to dance
with the syringes and you'll make sunrise . . . it can all be
done . . . a man's perception can encompass entire planets,
force them to operate in certain ways . . . very easily, just a
small shift . . . a man's perception will alter trajectories, will
force microcosms to collide . . . just a small shift . . .
collision/prepare for impact/and clash . . . like titans, like

bullet trains, like the mad gazelles of Africa drinking from the
bounty of the *grachten* . . . we fade out with a handshake and
a promise of words . . .

❧ BAILING WATER

we were traveling the Seine
we were walking through the mall
sitting at a bar, we were
bailing
    water

we were sleeping on the beach
we were kissing on a train
playing in the dark, we were
bailing

lost in New York
we dreamt of San Diego
    water

and lost in San Diego
we had dreams of Mexico
bailing
made Mexico a year later and we bought two pails
hopped onto the sand and
we kicked off our shoes
and we rolled up our pants and
started
bailing
    water

೧ KAHLEEB

Ashraf poured two glasses of wine and sat down. Across from
him sat Kahleeb, the friend, the war hero, the genius and one
time right hand man to the president of Egypt. The year was
1976. The temperature was 68 degrees. The sun was going
down somewhere over Cairo and they both took a sip of
wine. Ashraf pulled out a package of small, hand rolled cigars
with a caricature of Nefertitti on the cover, lit one, and
offered the pack. Kahleeb accepted.
They sat, smoking, and absorbed in thought. Ashraf thought
about his wife. 10 years of marriage, 2 children, both males, 2
cars, both Peugeots, and one sex life, non-existent. He opened
his mouth.

"Kahleeb, I no longer know what to do. I love Widad, I
always have, but the situation just seems to be getting worse."
"How so?"
"I come home from work - there's no dinner. The fridge is
filled with dirt - rotten fruit and meat. My sons wear dirty
diapers. Shit! I have no idea what to do with her. She doesn't
even like to be fucked anymore."
"No?"
"Listen to this, I put the children to sleep and I ask her, you
know, how about a little action tonight."
"And?"
"And she pretends to be sleeping, but I know she's not
sleeping because of the way she's breathing. It's not regular,
you know, and it drives me crazy. We haven't fucked in
almost a year."

They finished the cigars and stubbed them out in the ashtray.
Kahleeb was thinking about futility. Human relationships,
procreation, the art of love, the art of war, murder,
prostitution, donations to charity, soccer scores, emphysema-
existence and accomplishment, the art futility. He took a sip
of the wine.

"Well, Ashraf, there's only one solution I can think of."

"What's that?"

"You should rape her."

"What?"

"You heard me. Rape her. It's the only way. Come home and put the kids to sleep and rape her."

"I could never do that."

"Why not?"

"Well, she'd scream."

"Then gag her."

"And she'd fight me off."

"Fight you off? You're stronger than she is. And if she starts giving you trouble, well, all you have to do is hit her."

"No Kahleeb, I wouldn't be able to do something like that."

"Yes you would. You just underestimate yourself. But it's alright. That's what men do."

"Huh?"

"It's almost impossible for a man to realize his capabilities until he's faced with an extreme situation. The next time you see her pretending to be asleep take off your belt and really lay into her. Give her one on the ass if she's got her back to you, and if not, then work her thighs."

"I could never do that."

"Then you'll never be happy with her."

"What about aphrodisiacs? There's gotta be something."

"Look, I'm your friend, I wouldn't tell you to do something unless I was sure of it. If you give her an aphrodisiac then you might have her that one night, but if you rape her, then she will never say no to you. She'll be too scared."

"And what about the children?"

"Send them away. Send them to a neighbor's house."

"Do you really think it will work?"

"I know it will. Rape her two or three times and she'll start coming around. The legs will spread, dinner will be served, food will be in the fridge and your children will be spotless."

"Are you serious?"

"Yes. More wine?"

Ashraf stood up and walked towards the kitchen, produced a bottle of wine, poured two glasses, walked away from the kitchen, and sat down. Across from him sat Kahleeb, the friend, the war hero, the genius and one time right hand man to the president of Egypt. 1976. The temperature had dropped down to 55 degrees and the sun had disappeared somewhere over Cairo. They both took a sip of wine. Ashraf pulled out the cigars, lit one, and offered the pack. Kahleeb accepted. Kahleeb was thinking about raping Ashraf's wife and the thought depressed him. This whole thing depressed him. Everything depressed him: futility and rape and friendship and the war, belts and children and medals of honor, all of it - every thing, every where, every body, depressing.

"Ashraf."
"Yes."
"If you don't rape her, then I'll do it."
"What?"
"You heard me, if you don't rape her, then I'll do it myself. I'll come by one day while you're at work and I'll take off my belt and begin to . . . "
"What the hell is wrong with you!"
"Nothing. I'm only trying to help."
"How are you trying to help?"

Kahleeb didn't answer. He remained silent for a few minutes and thought about the futility of silence. Being silent is like being out on the ocean and bailing water, he thought, and what's the point, the rain is bound to come, some dam is bound to break, earthquakes, volcanoes, the shifting of tectonic plates, something, anything sooner or later and then what? Huh? Float away on conversation? Build an ark out of chitchat? An Atlantis of jabber-monkeys equipped with megaphones, swinging from trees and reciting Plato? What? Ashraf stood up to leave.

"Ashraf, just think about it."
"I don't have to think about it. It's a sick thought."
"Look, I can understand that being your initial reaction . . . "
"Just stay away from my wife, Kahleeb. I'm being serious."
"And so am I. I'll call you in a week. If by that time you still haven't raped her . . ."

Ashraf slammed the door on his way out. Kahleeb stood up

and walked towards the kitchen, poured a glass of wine, walked away from the kitchen, and sat back down. Kahleeb, the friend, the war hero, the genius and one time right hand man to the president of Egypt thought about Ashraf and his wife and of rape and of belts. Futility. 1976.
50 degrees and there was a full moon, somewhere over Cairo.

CR I'VE COME TO THE FOLLOWING CONCLUSION

(which is?) That you will never learn to hate your fellow man totally and indiscriminately until you've done the Manhattan rush hour commute. (to where?) To anywhere. Doesn't matter what your destination is. Get on that platform and you're surrounded by a minimum of 80 characters. 80 faceless, eyeless, soulless, mindless and degenerate characters and every last one of them a killer, a murderer, a vampire, an alien with death rays pouring from every rotten orifice on it's body and the focus of this energy is to custom create for you (for me?) (yes!) a waking, breathing and torturously endless hell of sweat and bustle. (that's pretty) And when I said 'every last one of them' I meant, (what?) EVERY LAST ONE OF THEM - the old women reek of cabbage and powders, medical ointments and anal creams; the young women reek of perfume and makeup, engagement rings and herpes; the children are bouncing balls, shitting pants, yelling, running, singing with urine streaked yellow voices and grinning dark chocolate grins; the old men are farting and playing cards, wearing suites and neckties, thinking of hemorrhoids, stock options, gas prices, fingering young secretaries and golf and fishing; the Mexicans eat tacos, carry crabs and tool boxes; the teenyfucks are loud, they talk loud and they laugh loud and they're talking about nothing and they're laughing at nothing; the construction workers snore, the black girls curse, the perverts rub, the mothers attend and the conductor's a drunk (shit!) and this is something you actually have to pay for! (no) (yeah) I pay about a hundred and seventy dollars a month to get shuttled around like this. I've been doing it for 2 years and there's 52 weeks a year at 5 days a week at 2 train rides a day at 50 minutes per train ride! Shit! 52,000 minutes with this crowd of jackals, vultures, hyenas and scavengers. I pay for this! I take the cash, which is deposited in my account at the first of every month by some great and unknown beast in exchange for my acting like a zombie, and I in turn deposit that cash into a machine with buttons and lights and ink and some sort of electrical intelligence which in turn prints a card that I hand to the red nosed, heavy drinking conductor so that he can punch holes in it. (makes sense) The heat's broken during the winter and there's no air conditioning in the summer. The seats are vinyl made to feel like leather. (that sounds nice) The seats feel like leather and are crisscrossed with duct tape to keep their insides inside and the tape sticks to your clothes, leaves a streak of adhesive on your back thus allowing you to stick to everything you come into contact with and allowing everything to stick to you. Sometimes you have to put a piece of paper down first so as not to ruin your pants. (hmmm) And sometimes there are suspicious looking stains on the seats so you have to think twice about sitting. (why is that?) (because) Who knows what those stains are? Who knows where they came from? (huh?) They could've leaked out of anybody! Out of anything! (anything?) Yes, some of the creatures that you see on the train defy any and all attempts at classification. They have trunks and growths, warts, dripping fluids, tentacles, they walk on 4 legs, 2 legs, 3 legs, some come slithering like eels, some come covered in latex, some are even packaged in boxes and bear post office stamps so as to avoid paying the train fare. (wow!) Yeah, and after you've dealt with this scenario for any length of time you find that you would just as soon turn a flamethrower on these people/animals/aliens/vampires as you would help them off the pavement if they were to slip on a patch of ice/spilled motor oil/banana peel/used condom. You start to have homicidal fantasies. You begin saving up for a rifle. You spend your train ride daydreaming of Molotov cocktails, electrocution, firing squads and chugging beer. (beer?) You

drink a half-gallon of beer so that the mind reaches such a
numb point of incoherence allowing you to maintain a
certain, um, decorum, or better yet, a state of indifference. A
better author once said something to the following effect:
people get hurt/mad/depressed/offended only because they
care too much. If you learn not care about anything then
nothing will be able hurt/madden/depress/offend you. I
haven't learned to do this, yet. I still care too much. (about
what?) But what it is that I care about I haven't figured out,
yet. So instead I get a kick in the ass to jump-start me on my
road to indifference. I pour 64 fluid ounces of domestic beer
directly down the throat as if in an attempt to drown myself.
(your self?) But in reality, I'm drowning out everyone else.
It's an escape hatch - a security measure - a surefire way to
ignore the death rays and tentacles and send me speedily
along to where I need to be - permits me to deal with every
second of those 52,000 minutes like some golden and shiny
prince valiant type of commuter. (are you serious?) (yes) I tell
the anal cream old women, 'Go right ahead ma'am, I was just
saving the seat for you.' I smile at the children and wink at
the Mexicans, let the perverts get a feel as we shuffle up the
aisle. I laugh with the old men as they scream about rotten
poker hands. I even hold the door open for the young ladies
so that they can squeeze their engagement rings and herpes
sores onto the train a little easier. And the whole time, while
I'm smiling, winking, laughing helping, humping, holding, in
my head, like a mantra, ' . . . every one of you dead. If I had
only one wish I would use it to vaporize the entire lot of you
right out of existence . . . every one of you dead.' (seems
rather harsh) It makes me happy, thinking like that, and I
analyze all this and think to myself, if the thought of
everyone being dead makes me so happy, then I myself might
have a problem. (maybe) Maybe my problem is the same as
all the other people's problems and all the other people's
problems are a mirror image of my own. (maybe) Maybe we
all hate each other and maybe we all daydream of some mass
homicidal act that will give us just a little peace, just a little
quiet, just some downtime after being made to dance all day
for supervisors that shoot at our feet and take extended

vacations. Maybe. And I look around at the crowd on the platform. I take in their odd shaped bodies and their faceless faces. I freeze a snapshot in my mind and then I go home and look in the mirror. I compare the two images. (and?) Shit! I come to the conclusion, that there's absolutely no difference.

℃ℛ MAN

man wants a nice car
schooling
strains his neck, doesn't mind licking superiors, ambitious
wants a good,
clean wife,
the type who'll cry in the shower after being given orgasms in the most fiendish
of ways, wants a nice
two story, maybe even on the water
children
promotions
sexual fantasy vacation, send jr. off to summer camp and
charge the wife with a rhinoceros horn . . . picked the thing up on Ebay,
takes two C batteries.

man wants security
southern comfort sedation and predictable afternoons, 401k, low risk retirement fund,
3 percent growth and dinner with colleagues, owns a small handgun, sure,
let me guess,
also watches professional wresting, masturbates with his eyes open and sends the missus out for laundry detergent while the Raiders run up-field.

I meet this redhead at a bar on Long Island.
Man bumps into her.
Spills a drink on her shirt and walks away.
Man doesn't apologize.

She says, "Aren't you gonna do something?"
"It'll take too much effort." I tell her.
"Too much effort?"
"Yeah."
"Huh, a real man would do something."
"Maybe."
"Well, maybe you're not a real man then." And I take the
compliment pretty well, real graceful, kind of swan like and I
smile, while thinking about all the real men out there. I wave
over the bartender, put down a 20-dollar bill.
"I'll settle my tab," then motioning at the redhead, "and I've
got her next drink."

I get up,
and walk out,
still smiling, I hadn't felt that good in years.

ℭℛ THE MAIN PROBLEM

The main problem
is that you have no REAL way of knowing -
(knowing what?)
- whether or not your writing two-bit bullshit,
or if you're really laying it down, the way it's meant to be,
but then you ask your self: What
is it MEANT to be?
Is it MEANT to be anything - anything at all?

And there's no answers, there's smoke up your ass and
rejection letters from places like The Burning Word, or
maybe
The Oyster Boy Review, and you read the letters and say:

Fuck,
those rags wouldn't know lit if it wore a red dress, hopped on
their laps, and showed much cleavage -

or you say:

Fuck,

those guys know all about lit and I'm just some cross dresser
in red, hopping on laps, and showing silicone cleavage -

But then you think:

Wait a minute; I've got a collection of poetry coming out, and
don't forget the little Greek magazine, or that anthology
printed in India, or that Leon the editor say's I'm first in line
once the presses are up and running or that I had that column
for a few
sweet months, or,
or,
Fuck! Those guys at Oyster Boy really DO know all about lit
and I'm definitely some cross dresser in a secondhand skirt,
hopping on laps, and showing Kleenex cleavage - Hey
everybody,
look! A snake swallowing its tail!
That's the shape of these thoughts; a self-destructive circle
that spins real vicious
and always ends
real bloody.

Obviously, there's no set path to take.
No equation to follow.
No
A character meets B story line that will give you the big C
(cunt
maybe? yeah, definitely,
cunt - the big C) of literature. It just doesn't happen. Now,
I'm not denying the existence of the 'Best Seller' equation. I
know it's out there. Just look for it, you won't be
disappointed. What I'm getting at is something else.

If you really want to CREATE
something new, something different and unheard of,
something
that hasn't even crossed the minds of the greats,
you have to put YOUR balls
out on the line.

DON'T
follow dance diagrams on how to move like Vonnegut

because you'll only jig
a cheap imitation.

DON'T
read cookbook recipes on how to bake like Burroughs
because you'll only burn
your microwave dinner.

And DON'T
study the manual on how to wash windows like Fante,
you'll punch your hand through the glass and realize one
thing:

(oh yeah - and what's that one thing Johnny? huh? c'mon
smart ass, let's hear it.)
(you sure you wanna hear it? can't say it's real positive or
anything.)
(just fucken spill it already, your losing the reader!)
(o.k., o.k. fucker, here it is, but remember, you asked for it.)

You realize that you don't like the color of your own blood-
and that's just depressing shit. Really,
very depressing shit. What happens when you see that
your guts're weak and that your words're rotten?
The Big Empty comes on - that's what. The Escape Dream
seems like a pretty picture and you wanna paint yourself onto
the canvas. Buy the one-way ticket. Or maybe you pull a
Nick Cage in Leaving Las Vegas, bottles drained and
carpeting
the floor.

But that takes guts.
Do you have em?

Ah - FUCK!

The friends are no help -
You can learn more from your enemies.

The women are no help -
You either work to kill them or they work to kill you.
And you have no heroes to look up to,
the ones that had spark and flare at the beginning have taken
university teaching jobs or live off grants, somewhere in

Seattle. Some have been screwed by fan mail and ego. And
some have been screwed
by LIFE
itself.

Now they pump out soft words or no words, or no, no,
nothing - nothing at all, just empty thoughts, bound in
hardcover, compliments of the
Ihaveanameandallineedtodoistypeandsubmitandsitbackcollect
ingroyalties Incorporated Press.

So
what do you do about it? Well,
what CAN you do? Not read?

Of course not,

- you need the reading, you need to see the style out there,
dissect/learn from it, find out how/why it works when it does,
see who the big players are, figure how to beat them, if you
can beat them, how to set yourself APART FROM THEM.
That's major! Who wants to pick up something and say
'hmmm . . . writes just like Kafka.' Or 'striking resemblance
to the work Thompson.'

Shit,
if people want Kafka - they go to the library and pick up The
Metamorphosis,
and if they want Thompson - they get The Rum Diaries.
Meanwhile,
you're pushing a dirty mop across THEIR clean floor,
hiding under THEIR dinner table with a notepad, in order to
pick up crumbs,
Shit!
You wind up smoking the half cigarettes that fall from the
mouths of your idols and spread shit eating grin across plastic
face and that
just doesn't
cut it.

But let's say you're able to squeeze OUT of the mold, let's
say you're typing wild, WILD shit with no trace of the carbon

· 200 ·

paper, then what? Then you have to maintain it and that's
twice as hard as the initial creation. You can catch record
weight marlin everyday for a week and feel like a champ.
Then one day you toss your line overboard and get nothing.
You come home empty handed and broken. You see that the
lows carry more weight than the highs. They beat shit, piss,
and hell out of your confidence; leave you clutching cheap
memories and toying with deathbed ideas. You sit there
screaming 'what a rigged fucken game' at the walls and
ceiling. You ask 'Which side of the coin is better?' And you
figure out: either way you bet
it's heavy
and the odds
are always against you.

So then, why the hell do you do it? Why do you drop friends
and family and a nice healthy future in corporate America
with the semi-attractive wife and two story house with gas
guzzling, imported car in the driveway?

Because it's all you know - and it may sound pitiful, being
born with opportunity out the ass, good parents and happy
childhood, college degree, high IQ and all the rest, but the
only thing you really care about, all you feel for and chase
after, is the art of stringing one word after the other. That's it.
Screw science, screw math,
screw the information superhighway and while you're at it,
toss prison bar religion out the fifth floor window.
Screw friends and social gatherings where the band plays
your old time favorites.
Screw the future and the Fourth of July and the christening of
other people's babies in
Catch-22
Chinese
finger cuff type churches where priests run mad with the
young boy itch and the holy water is blessed by pedophilic
hands.
Screw it!
Screw the fact that you can pick up a phone, right now,
and convince three different women

to spread long legs
and let you in
for the long ride - Don't you get it?
It means nothing when the one that you DO love
lives only 5 blocks away,
but she could be in Dallas with an oil millionaire, back seat,
of a black limousine,
drinking champagne
and smiling real pretty, for all the time
she'd give you.
Screw it!

You just type

through the self destruct thoughts
through the sexless nights
through the empty bottles and 750 milligrams of street corner
vicodin

You just type

and it's for an audience of one
for a single critic
for that one reviewer
you have to look in the eye every morning

that one mother who knows your dirty secrets and your
hidden fantasies,
the one you carry around in your mind
through piss
and fuck
and anarchy
and shit lifestyle
and razor's edge existence so that when it's time for the final
punch out, and you collect that big paycheck, you can say to
yourself
'Now this
is some honest fucking money.'

                                             - John